Justin Morgan Had a Horse

by MARGUERITE HENRY

Inside illustrations by WESLEY DENNIS

SCHOLASTIC INC.
New York Toronto London Auckland Sydney
Mexico City New Delhi Hong Kong Buenos Aires

To my Morgan horse, Friday,
and to Fred Tejan, who gentled him

ISBN-13: 978-0-545-00556-2
ISBN-10: 0-545-00556-6

12 11 10 9 8 7 6 5 4 3 2 1   7 8 9 10 11/0

Printed in the U.S.A.   40

This edition first printing, January 2007

CONTENTS

For their help the author is grateful to

WALTER B. MAHONY, great-great-grandson of JUSTIN MORGAN
FANNIE S. GOSS, granddaughter of JOEL GOSS
F. B. HILLS, Secretary, The Morgan Horse Club
Vermont Historical Society
DR. PAUL O. McGREW, Chicago Natural History Museum
HELEN HARTNESS FLANDERS, Archivist for Vermont Traditional Music
The Chicago Public Library
Fletcher Free Library, Burlington, Vermont
St. Johnsbury Athenaeum, St. Johnsbury, Vermont
The Library of the University of Vermont
State of Vermont Reference Bureau at Montpelier
Fiske Foundation Library, Claremont, New Hampshire
The late DR. C. J. ATTIG, Head of History, North Central College
The late DAVID DANA HEWITT, Vermont pioneer

Foreword

THIS IS THE STORY of a common, ordinary little work horse who turned out to be the father of a famous family of American horses. He lived in the Green Mountain country of Vermont in the days when America was growing up. In fact, he helped it grow up. He dragged logs and cleared the land. He helped build the first log houses. He helped build bridges and cut roads through the wilderness.

Even in his own lifetime, the willingness of this little horse became an American legend. He labored hard all day, and then at sundown, when he should have been fed and bedded down for the night, he took part in races and pulling bees. He could walk faster, trot faster, run faster, and pull heavier logs than any other horse in all Vermont!

Today his descendants, known as Morgan horses, are renowned throughout the world. Yet nobody knows whether that first Morgan's parents were British or French or Dutch. And nobody really cares. As Joel Goss figured it out: "He's just like us. He's American. That's what he is! American!"

M.H.

Joel Meets Little Bub

THE LITTLE reddish-brown colt stopped nibbling grass. He lifted his head high and sniffed the noonday wind. His nostrils fluttering, he sniffed again. Long, quivering sniffs. A man and a boy were coming up the road. They must have journeyed a long way, for their man smell was almost blotted by dust.

Now the colt whinnied sharply. Instantly a bigger colt, scratching at a greenhead fly, alerted. He alerted so suddenly it seemed as if his name had been called out. He trotted over to the little colt, touching noses with him. Then his ears pricked as he caught the sound of booted feet walking slowly, and of bare feet running. Now he, too, knew that strangers were coming up the road.

Wearily, wearily the man's steps dragged. As he reached the fence, he rested his arms on the top rail and his whole body seemed to go limp. The boy leaned against the fence too, but not from weariness. His was an urgent desire to get close to the colts. The boy's blue linsey-woolsey shirt was faded and torn, and his breeches, held up by a strip of cowhide, were gray with dust. His stubbly hair was straw-colored, like a cut-over field of wheat. Everything about him looked dry and parched. Everything except his eyes. They peered over the fence with a lively look, and his tongue wet his dry lips.

"You!" he said with a quick catch of his breath, as the littler colt came over and gazed curious-eyed at him. "I could gentle you, I could."

The man sighed. "We're here at last, Joel. We can put our bundles down and rest a spell before we see if Farmer Beane's at home."

The boy had not heard. He just stood on tiptoe, holding his bundle and gaping at the colts as if he had never seen their like before. "That little one . . ." he whispered.

Just then a door slammed shut, and from the house beyond the meadow a farmer in his working clothes started down a footpath toward them. "How-de-do!" he called out as he came closer. Two rods' distance from them, he shaded his eyes and stared intently.

With a whistle of surprise he stopped in his tracks. "Great Jumping Jehoshaphat!" he shouted. "If it ain't Justin Morgan, schoolmaster and singing teacher! Why, I'm as pleasured to see you as a dog with two tails." He set down a bucket he was carrying and shook hands across the fence. "Who's the fledgling you got with you?" he asked, pointing a thumb toward the boy.

"This lad is Joel Goss, one of my scholars. I board with his parents," the schoolmaster explained. "And when I mentioned that I'd be going off on a junket till school starts, I could see he wanted to traipse along. Joel," he said, putting his hand on the boy's shoulder, "I'd like you to meet Farmer Beane, an old neighbor of mine."

Reluctantly Joel turned from the colts to face the farmer. He had never been introduced before. It made him blush to the roots of his sunburnt hair.

"Cat got your tongue, boy?" the farmer said, not unkindly. "Or be you smitten on the colts?" And without waiting for an answer, he popped more questions. "Where in tarnation you two come from? You hain't come all the ways from Randolph, Vermont, to Springfield, Massachusetts, be you?"

Justin Morgan nodded.

"Sakes alive! You must be all tuckered out. Why,

9

even as the crow flies, it's over a hundred mile down here. You didn't walk the hull way, I hope."

The schoolmaster took off his hat and ran his fingers through graying hair. "Yes, Abner; that is, most all the way, except when Lem Tubbs and his team of oxen gave us a short haul into Chicopee."

"Well, gosh all fishhooks, let's not stand here a-gabbin'. Come in, come in! The woman'll give us hot cakes and tea. I'll bet Joel here could do with some vittles. He's skinny as a fiddle string. Come in, and by and by we can chat."

All during the conversation the colts had been inching closer and closer to Farmer Beane. Now they were nipping at his sleeves and snuffing his pockets.

"These tarnal critters love to be the hull show," chuckled the farmer, reaching into his pockets. "If I don't bring 'em their maple sugar, the day just don't seem right to them. Nor to me, neither."

Justin Morgan steadied himself against the fence. "Abner," he said, "before Joel and I sit down to your table, it seems I should tell you why I've come." He paused, nervously drumming the top rail for courage. After a while he looked up and his glance went beyond the meadow and the rolling hills. "I've come," he swallowed hard, "because I've a need for the money you owed me when I moved away to Vermont."

There was a moment of silence. It was so still that

10

the colts munching their sugar seemed to be very noisy about it. Joel thought of the bright red apple he had eaten last night. He wished now that he had saved it for them.

It was a long time before the farmer could answer. Then he said, "You've come a terrible long way, Justin, and 'tis hard for me to disappoint you. But me and the woman have had nothin' but trouble." He began counting off his troubles on his fingers: "Last year, my cows got in the cornfield and et theirselves sick and died; year afore that, the corn was too burned to harvest; year afore that, our house caught afire. I just hain't got the money."

Master Morgan's shoulders slumped until his homespun coat looked big and loose, as if it had been made for someone else. "I'd set great store on getting the money," he said. "I've got doctor bills to pay and . . ." He took a breath. "For years I've been hankering to buy a harpsichord for my singing class."

There! The words were out. He spanked the dust from his hat, then put it back on his head and forced a little smile. "Don't be taking it so hard, Abner. I reckon my pitch pipe can do me to the end of my days." His voice dropped. "And maybe that won't be long; I feel my years too much."

The farmer pursed his lips in thought. "Justin," he said, "I ain't a man to be beholden to anyone. Would you take a colt instead of cash?"

Joel wheeled around to see if Mister Beane was in earnest.

"Now this big feller, this Ebenezer," the farmer was saying as he pointed to the bigger colt, "he's a buster! He'll be a go-ahead horse sure as shootin'. If you looked all up and down the Connecticut Valley, I bet you couldn't find a sensibler animal." He glanced at the schoolmaster's set face and spoke more persuasively. "Besides, he's halter broke! He'd be the very horse to ride to school."

Justin Morgan shook his head. "No, Abner, I'm but a stone's throw from school, and a colt would just mean another mouth to feed."

"Why, bless my breeches," the farmer laughed hollowly, "if you ain't a-goin' to use him, you could sell him long afore you run up a feed bill. Already the river folk got their eye on him. He'll fetch a pocketful of money. Mebbe twice as much as I owed you!"

The schoolmaster studied his dust-covered boots as if he did not want to look at Ebenezer.

"By Jove," the farmer added, "I'll even give you a premium. I'll throw in Little Bub for good measure."

Joel tugged at the schoolmaster's coattails. "Please, sir!" His eyes begged. "I could . . ."

" 'Course, he ain't the colt Ebenezer is," Mister Beane went on. "He's just a mite of a thing. But there's *something* about those two! They stay to-

12

gether snug as two teaspoons. Scarcely ever do you see one alone." The farmer spoke more hurriedly now, as if the rain of words might convince where reasons failed. "Eb's kind of like a mother to Bub. Why, I've seen Bub nip Ebenezer on the flank, and that big colt knew 'twas just in fun! He'd turn right around and nuzzle the little one. If'n you didn't know, you'd actually think the colt was his'n!"

Master Morgan laughed a dry laugh, like wind rustling through a cornfield. "I don't need two horses any more than I need water in my hat! They would be *two* more mouths to feed."

Joel broke in timidly. "I reckon I could feed and gentle Little Bub?" he pleaded.

The schoolmaster's eyes smiled down at the boy, ignoring the question. "In the hills of Vermont," he said kindly, "farmers want big, strong oxen. Not undersized cobs like Bub."

The smaller colt stood so close to the fence now that Joel reached out and touched the tremulous nose. It felt like plush.

"Ee-magine that!" clucked the farmer. "The little nipper didn't even snort. Your Joel's got a way with him, he has. Wouldn't wonder if he *could* gentle the critter."

He turned to Ebenezer now and picked up his feet, first one and then another. "Look-a-here, Justin, see how mannerly this feller is! As a schoolmaster, you know good dispositions from bad." Next he

13

pressed Ebenezer's muscles, and then lifted his upper lip to show the strong teeth.

At last he turned to the little colt. "Ye're right about this 'un," he said. "Bub *is* only pint measure. But he's mannerly, too. Except . . ." He hesitated. "Yep, I may as well tell ye — 'cept when he sees a dog. He can't abide 'em! They make him mad as any hornet. He strikes out at 'em with his feet, and squeals and chases 'em until they go lickety-split for home, tails tucked clean under their bellies."

Joel laughed in glee, as if he could see the whole performance.

But Justin Morgan stood grave and silent. "Perchance," he said at last, "you are right, Abner. Perchance in Vermont I can sell Ebenezer. But the little fellow would be just a worry to me. It's kind of you to offer them both, but you keep Little Bub."

Abner Beane grasped the schoolmaster's hand and shook it heartily. "The bargain is sealed," he said. "And now let's go in and eat!"

A Fuzzy Shadow

EARLY THE NEXT MORNING Joel stirred on his straw mattress, listening to the exciting sounds of the new day — birds making little twittering remarks, a cock crowing lustily, calves bawling.

Then for a while there was silence, except for the steady breathing of the schoolmaster, who lay sleeping beside him.

Joel drowsily wondered where he was. He opened his eyes, expecting to see a leafy roof over his head.

But in the half darkness he saw beams and cross-beams, like his bedroom ceiling at home.

Suddenly he was sharp awake. He held his breath, straining to hear a far-off sound — a high, quavering whinny that ended in a snorty rumble.

Now Joel knew! He was at Farmer Beane's! He sank cozily into the straw, letting little shivers of happiness race up and down his spine. In imagination he was in the meadow — stroking Little Bub's neck, now slipping a halter over his nose, now leading him to some green paradise where there was no talk of money or debts. He raised up gingerly, trying to keep the straw in the mattress from crackling. If he was careful not to make any noise, he might steal out of doors and be alone with Little Bub. Even a few minutes alone would be fun.

Slowly, slowly he sat up, then slid his feet out of bed and to the floor. He felt for his clothes, slipped into his shirt and pulled on his breeches, hitching them up with the strip of cowhide.

He waited a moment or two, making sure the schoolmaster's breathing was still steady. Then he tiptoed for the ladder and swung silently down the rungs and into the candle-lit kitchen.

Mistress Beane was bent double over the hearth, poking in among the ashes. "That you, Joel?" she asked, taking out a stone crock.

"Yes'm."

With an "Oh, me" and an "Oh, my" Mistress

Beane got to her feet, using the mantel to hoist herself up. "I hearn as how the schoolmaster's feeling poorly," she said, "so I made him some of my Indian meal porridge. It'll stick to his ribs on that long journey home."

Joel edged toward the door.

"Oh, no, you don't!" the woman called. "Man or boy, you got to eat, too. I declare! I never seed two such puny critters."

She spooned some porridge into a big brown bowl and poured hot butter and milk over it. "You buckle right down and eat. It'll make you lively as pepper the hull day long."

Joel began to eat rapidly, while his eyes kept darting from the bowl in front of him to a basket of red apples in the center of the table.

"Good years or bad, we most always has apples," Mistress Beane said, following Joel's glance. "And land knows when you'll get your next meal. Help yourself to as many as you can carry."

Joel tried to say his thanks, but the porridge stuck in his throat.

"You've et enough, son. If it won't down, it won't. Mebbe you'd like to hightail it outdoors and find Mister Beane. He'll be milking 'long about now, and there's some mighty purty kittens to play with in the barn."

Joel neatly stacked his dishes. Then he selected two of the biggest and ripest apples, thanked Mis-

17

tress Beane shyly, and hurried out into the gray morning.

He spied the colts at once. Down at the far end of the meadow they were stretched out in a joyous run, their tails floating on the wind. Gulping a deep breath, Joel went racing in the dew to meet them. He tried to shout to them, to call their names, but the wind rushed at him, smothering his voice.

At sight of the oncoming figure the two colts slowed, then halted altogether. Their eyes studied the boy, and the very air seemed charged with suspense.

"Now is the time," Joel said to himself. "Now!" He took the apples from inside his shirt and, slowly moving closer, offered one on the palm of each hand. Ebenezer eyed them but a moment. Then he came forward and nimbly helped himself. Little Bub, however, danced away, snorting. Joel made no move to follow. He stood very still, waiting. The little colt snorted again, as if daring Joel to come a step closer. Then curiosity got the better of him. Besides, he could hear Ebenezer crunching the apple, and he could smell its sweetness. His feet moved nearer, one tiny hoof, then another.

At last the quick breath on Joel's hand, and the funny little whiskers tickling his fingers. Then Bub lifted the apple, and in that moment boy and colt were friends.

Joel's heart seemed to catch in his throat. "I wish

18

'twas you that was coming along," he said softly. "Ebenezer — well, he's nice enough; but you and me, we could grow big *together!*"

Joel and Little Bub were so lost in a delightful world of their own that they both shied as Master Morgan and Farmer Beane approached.

Stepping quietly and carefully, the schoolmaster now walked up to Ebenezer. With the farmer's help he eased a halter over the big colt's head and fastened a short rope to it. Then he turned to Joel.

"Here, son, you take the lead rope. You can guide Ebenezer on our homeward journey. Farmer Beane was right. You've a way with horses, I do believe."

Joel's hands made no move.

"Say good-bye to Bub now." The tired voice was filled with regret.

Joel bit his lower lip to stop its trembling. Without a word he faced away from Little Bub. He took the lead rope in his clenched fist and led Ebenezer through the gate. His footsteps faltered and his small, resolute chin seemed to say, "I could take care of Bub, too. I could."

As soon as Joel and Ebenezer were on the other side of the fence, the schoolmaster blocked the open gate so that Little Bub could not escape. He turned now to shake hands with the farmer. "I know you've done the best you could about the debt, Abner."

"And I'm obliged to you for crossing it off, Justin. 'Twas extraordinary nice of you to put it in writing. I always did say you was the most elegant writer in the state of Massachusetts."

Now the good-byes were said, and there was no delaying any longer. The boy slid his fingers through Ebenezer's halter strap and headed him northward. The sun was pointing thin fingers of gold above the horizon.

"Good-bye, Little Bub," Joel's lips said. He cast a troubled glance backward, and suddenly his heart began hammering wildly. Farmer Beane had not closed the gate! He was actually standing aside, letting the colt push past him.

"Hey, Justin!" cried the farmer. "The little one — he wants to tag along. Better take him for the lad."

The early morning light made a fuzzy shadow of Little Bub as he came pattering straight across the road to Ebenezer.

Joel smothered a cry of joy. He was almost afraid to breathe. He looked neither to the right nor to the left. His bare feet sank noiselessly into the dust. "Please, God," he whispered, "don't let Little Bub turn back. Please, God, don't let him turn back."

But Little Bub had no thought of turning back. He threw his head high and investigated the wind with all manner of snuffings and snortings. Then his delicate ears pointed this way and that to hear the small thunder of his own hoofbeats. At last he whisked his curly black tail. "I'm coming along!" he said, more plainly than if he had talked.

Justin Morgan looked at the young colt and frowned. Then he saw the happy tilt to the boy's head. He shrugged his shoulders. "All right, all right," he said helplessly.

Joel's excitement could not be held in. He let out a great sigh of happiness. Little Bub was his! There was no mistaking it now. At least for the long journey home, the colt was his!

Northward to Vermont

They were scarcely out upon the highroad when Master Morgan began teaching. Teaching was in his blood, and he couldn't help giving lessons along the way.

"Joel," he announced in his first-day-of-school voice, "we have two new pupils with us, and I'm of a mind to make this a pleasant junket. If we swing along at a nice easy pace, we should reach the village of Chicopee before the sun is over our heads.

That's where the little Chicopee River joins up with the big Connecticut. You remember how the Connecticut got its name, don't you, Joel?"

Joel nodded but said nothing as he led Ebenezer along and kept his eye on the caperings of Little Bub. He knew the answer well enough, but the way the schoolmaster told it made it more exciting.

"Boys!" the teacher was saying. "I want you to picture Indian braves shooting their boats over the rapids, calling out to each other: *'Quonnec! Quonnec!'* which means 'long,' and *'Tuck'* which means 'river.'"

Joel could almost see the brown bodies like arrows flashing through the spray. *"Quonnec-tuck* sounds fiercer and better than Connecticut," he offered.

"So it does!" the schoolmaster chuckled. He turned from the boy, and with a smile let his glance slide over the gangly colts. Now that they were his, he felt an inner squeeze of affection. He watched the dust rise from under their feet as they pranced along. "Ebenezer, Little Bub," he spoke quietly to them, "we'll be crossing a covered bridge soon. You two ever been on a bridge? Likely not. But you'll admire the sound of your hoofs clattering over wood. See if you don't!"

The colts pricked their ears to take in the schoolmaster's voice. It had a soft huskiness that seemed part of the wind and the river. And the way he

23

looked at them when he talked — it was as if they were all friends making a pilgrimage together.

"Along about twilight," the master went on, "we should be near enough to Hadley Falls to feel the spray on our faces. We'll have a fine feast there. Joel and I will catch pike or perch, while you two graze the delicious grass that grows on the banks. And it wouldn't surprise me if an obliging farmer would have a nosebag of corn to trade for the writing of a letter or the chanting of a psalm. Then we'll all bed down under the stars and let the music of the falls sing us to sleep."

And so, with pleasant talk, the morning spent itself. Noontide found them crossing the bridge at Chicopee, just as the schoolmaster said they would. And by sundown they were all in wading below Hadley Falls, the man and the boy fishing for their supper, the colts rolling in the water, sudsing themselves clean.

In the early mist of the next morning, they were on their way again. The road they traveled was no more than a path, winding its way among trees. Every so often the schoolmaster sat down on the ground and leaned against a tree to rest. This gave the colts a chance to eat the green shoots that came up through the forest duff and to scratch their itchy shoulders against the tree trunks. And it gave Joel time to ease his bundle of clothes onto Little Bub and acquaint him with the feel of something on his back.

One day, while going through a deep woods, they heard the ring of ax strokes and the grunting of horses bent to the pull. Ebenezer whinnied to his fellow creatures. Then Little Bub added a few high notes which ended in a low rumble.

Joel laughed, and when they came upon the men clearing the wilderness, he explained like some proud parent, "That bugling you heard was our Little Bub. He was trying to act like a grown-up horse."

They passed well-tilled country, too — wheat fields, and fields of Indian corn with yellow squash planted between the rows. And they passed meadow land with horned cattle grazing. And one morning they met a train of oxcarts. The very first driver pulled up to chat.

"Howdy, folks!" he said. "Smart big colt you got there." Then he pointed his whip toward Little Bub. "But that runty one . . ." He paused a moment, sizing him up more carefully. "Nope, that little feller don't look like he'll amount to much."

This was the first time a traveler compared the two colts, but it was not the last. Day after day as they journeyed northward toward Vermont, their fellow travelers admired Ebenezer and scoffed at Little Bub. A cobbler who joined up with them for a mile or two even offered to buy the big colt in trade for his lapstone and awl. But Master Morgan needed cobbler's tools even less than he needed a horse.

"Joel," the schoolmaster admitted after he had turned down another offer, "discouragement rides me. With one colt at heel and another running free, our return trip is slowed. Here it is almost pumpkin time, and school begins in a month. How long will it take us? Three weeks? Four?"

The schoolmaster expected no answer and got none. He was talking as if to himself. The added responsibility seemed to weary him. Anxious as he was to get home, he had to stop more and more often to rest in the shade. Joel, meanwhile, pulled burrs out of Little Bub's tail and mane. And then, if Master Morgan's head nodded in sleep, he began talking nonsense to Little Bub as if they were two boys with a secret all their own. To his delight, the thing he longed for most was happening. The colt was answering in funny little whickers.

"He's smart as a fox," Joel would tell the schoolmaster when he awoke. "Knows lots of things."

As the journey continued, Master Morgan had to agree that Bub was smart. Always it was the little colt who first sensed the presence of a snake and warned the others with a rattling of his own breath. And always it was the little colt whose ear first caught the faraway blowing of a conch shell call-

26

ing men from the fields into dinner. The sound reminded him of Farmer Beane's place, where mealtime for the family meant a handout for him, too — turnip tops or carrot greens, or even leftover applejohn. Now, far away from home, he was off like a bullet at the faintest sounding of the conch shell.

The others learned to follow eagerly, for his trail always led to a kitchen door, where the air was spicy with the smell of gingerbread baking, or the steaming fragrance of pork pie.

There the schoolmaster would remove his hat and sing in his softly husky voice:

> "So pilgrims on the scorching sand,
>   Beneath a burning sky,
> Long for a cooling stream at hand;
>   And they must drink or die."

Before he reached the second stanza, the doorstep swarmed with curious-eyed children. "Look, Ma!" the youngsters would shout to the mother, who now came out, wiping her hands on her apron. "See the colts, Ma! They be singing, too!"

It was true. Whenever Master Morgan hit a high note, Ebenezer neighed, and then Little Bub chimed in with a rumbling obbligato.

This sent the children into peals of laughter.

When the song was over, the farmwife would suddenly think of her baking and send her eldest in to mind it. Then she would insist that the master and the boy come into the kitchen for a good hot meal, while the colts were turned out to pasture.

As she watched her guests enjoy her cooking, she would compliment them. "Oh, 'twas a joyful noise to listen to your hymn-singing without its being the Sabbath day!"

"Joel, of course, knows," Master Morgan replied, "but I may as well tell you that I composed these anthems myself. And nothing pleasures me more than to sing them."

There were days, however, when the schoolmaster did not sing at all, days when the wind churned the dust and set him to coughing. Then he walked more slowly, trying to quiet his spasms, sometimes steadying himself against the big colt.

It was strange how Justin Morgan and Ebenezer drew together as the trip lengthened out. They both tired early and they both seemed fearful of the wild animals that prowled by night. At the first sign of dusk, their eyes probed the shadows for catamounts and wolves, and Ebenezer's nostrils flared to catch their scent.

"Time to build a fire and bed down," Master Morgan would say. Yet neither the man nor the big colt could sleep. The man sat up cross-legged, elbows on knees, head resting in his hands, while nearby the colt dozed standing up. The smallest sounds startled them — an acorn falling on dry leaves, the pitapat of rabbit feet, the whimpering of an owl.

Joel and Bub, however, were lulled by the soft voices of night. The little colt lay stretched out on his side, and gradually the boy edged nearer and nearer until soon he was curled snug against the colt's back. It felt warm and furry, and Bub did not seem to mind.

Morning found them both eager and ready for new adventure. Rain or hot sunshine beating down on their heads, steep trails, skimpy food — nothing discouraged them. It was Joel and Bub who set the pace, and Ebenezer and the schoolmaster who lagged behind.

But one noonday, a third of the way home, the schoolmaster was suddenly a man transformed. They had crossed the state line into Vermont, and almost miraculously he seemed to gain new strength from the familiar green hills. He could not stop talking about them.

"Boys!" he rejoiced, as he called his pupils to a halt. "Vermont is named for its mountains. From the French words, *vert* for green and *mont* for mountain."

He straightened up to his full height and took off his hat in salute. "Our first settlers made a grand ceremony of the christening," he said, a light of pride in his eye. "They climbed Mount Pisgah right over yonder, and from that lofty eminence they looked round about. What they saw pleased them: hills peopled with deer, and down below in the valleys a carpet of green threaded with silver streams and rushing brooks."

Joel sighed. He wished he could find the right words, too, for the things he felt. He half closed his eyes, so that he could see the little company of pioneers climbing up Mount Pisgah. He tried to make believe the schoolmaster's voice belonged to one of them.

" 'We are met here upon this mount,' " the teacher was reciting, " 'which is part of the spine of America, which holds together the terrestrial ball, and divides the Atlantic Ocean from the Pacific. We are met here, gentlemen, to dedicate this wilderness to God and to give it a worthy name. That name shall be *Vert Mont*, in token that her mountains and hills shall be ever green and shall never die.' "

The boy put his arm around Little Bub's neck, listening to the husky voice as it now quoted from the Bible:

"I will lift up mine eyes unto the hills . . ."

Joel knew what the next words would be, and in his mind he was riding on Bub's back, riding into the hills.

". . . from whence cometh my help,"

he sang joyously in chorus with the schoolmaster.

Horse-trader Hawkes

MAN AND BOY and colts all seemed to fit together now, and to feel at home in the green hills. On and on they went, past tiny towns perched high on mountain shoulders or nestled snug in the crook of a stream. Nearly always a church spire rose from the cluster of homes and sharpened itself against the sky.

They walked in the dark of woods and in the sunlight of farm clearings. They saw pigs wearing wood collars to keep them from rooting under fences and wriggling away. They saw flying squirrels leaping from tree to tree, and black bears eating butternuts, and brown weasels scuttling in the underbrush. They saw small lakes like polished mirrors, and fishermen in boats, and hawks gliding in for a landing.

They heard the bleating of sheep, and wild geese honking, and beavers slapping their tails against the water. They heard the military music of waterfalls and the cradlesong of brooks.

They clattered over bridges with the printed warning:

Walk Your Horses

"That's all we've *been* doing!" Master Morgan would say to Joel with a smile.

Occasionally they ferried across swift-flowing streams. Ebenezer was struck with terror at sight of a ferry. He had to be bribed with corn and pushed to get on. Then he stood stiff-legged and quivering until the trip was over. But Little Bub sauntered aboard as gaily as a youngster going on a picnic. One ferryman nudged Master Morgan and laughed, "It'll be sixpence apiece for you and the big colt, but I'll let the lad and the runt go over for twopence, same as a goat."

Through deep grass, across broken country, along the gravelly bed of creeks, uphill and downhill, the little procession ate up the slow miles. Six days a week they pushed and plodded. But on the Sabbath

they did not travel at all, for there was a law in Vermont forbidding it.

Instead, the schoolmaster and the boy found the nearest meetinghouse and tied the colts to the hitching rack. Then shyly they stepped inside the cool, musty building and joined the worshipers.

Crowded into a box pew, Joel tried to listen to the preacher's voice running on, but it lulled him like the faraway droning of a bumblebee. His thoughts wandered, lifting him out of doors. He was at the hitching rack with the colts, tied alongside the work horses and oxen that had brought wagonloads of families to church. And they were all nodding and dozing in the warm sunshine as if they had known each other forever.

During one drowsy sermon, the preacher suddenly brought his fist down with a bang, and the voice that had been so low exploded in a mighty roar:

> "Awake, thou that sleepest,
> For the day of salvation is nigh!"

Heads everywhere in the meetinghouse fairly jolted to attention, while in the churchyard Little Bub let out a high bugle with that funny little rumble afterward.

Joel had to smother his laughter, for the tithingman stood ready with his staff to tap anyone acting unseemly.

When the service was over at last, the worshipers greeted Master Morgan and Joel and often invited them to join in the noontide meal. "We figure you folks come a-traveling a good long ways," some motherly person would say. "You must be mighty hungry. Come! Follow us out under the elms."

Like a flock of hungry starlings, the congregation scattered on the church lawn. From picnic hampers came thick slices of ham, homemade cheese, and brown-bread sandwiches filled with a rich layer of apple butter.

The boy and the master always ate their fill, and afterward the same motherly person would wrap up a nice cold snack of leftovers for them to take along.

It took nearly a month to walk the hundred miles and more back home. The days were growing shorter, and to Joel the sun seemed far away and choosy. It picked out the blobs of scarlet sumac and the yellow maple leaves, and then hung a misty haze over the rest of the world.

Now that the trip was almost over, the schoolmaster had little to say. He seemed to need all of his strength to put one foot ahead of the other. It was on a frosty twilight in September that they came to the junction of the Connecticut and the White rivers.

"At last, we are almost home! At last, we leave the Connecticut!" the schoolmaster sighed, raising an arm in farewell. "When the Indians named it the Long River, they were right as a bonnet in church."

The thought of home put an uneasiness on Joel. His mother, he knew, would try to figure a way to keep the colts, but his father . . .

"See that house snuggled down close to the White River?" the schoolmaster asked.

"Which one?" Joel wanted to know as his eye took in the cluster of frame buildings.

"The shabby one with the splendid chimney."

"And smoke curling out of it?"

"The very one. My sister Eunice lives there, and she will give us a night's lodging. Then first thing in the morning, we'll go next door and see what Neighbor Hawkes thinks of the colts. He's a good judge of horseflesh, and a sharp trader. He may even want to buy them."

Fear struck at Joel's heart. "Couldn't you just sell Ebenezer?" he asked quickly. "Little Bub probably wouldn't fetch much, anyway."

The schoolmaster had not heard. "Chimney smoke and candlelight look mighty inviting to me," he murmured as he headed toward his sister's house, half leaning on Ebenezer.

That night Joel slept in a bed for the first time on the homeward trip. It was a trundle bed, so short that he had to make an S of his body, and even then his toes poked through the slats. He felt crowded in on himself, and in his sleep he kept hitching around, dreaming he was Little Bub stabled in a chicken coop belonging to Horse-trader Hawkes.

Hiram Hawkes was at breakfast the next morning when Master Morgan, Joel, and the colts appeared. He came out onto the stoop, wiping his mouth with the back of his hand.

"Jumping Aunt Minnie!" he gulped. "Yer sister and me begun to think you two was never coming back, and here you be with two colts to boot."

Master Morgan stood twisting the frayed ends of Ebenezer's lead rope. His eye caught Joel's, then looked away. "What do you think of them?" he asked politely.

Hawkes squinted. He approached the animals cautiously, taking care to keep well out of kicking range. He circled one at a time. Then he stood with his own spindly legs braced far apart.

"Wal, now, Morgan," he drawled as he played with the watch chain looped across his paunch, "I'd say the big feller looks fair to middling, just fair to middling. But that little cob — he won't be worth no more than five dollar. Not even when he's growed. Legs too short, for one thing. He just ain't strung up right, Morgan. Now you've asked, and I've give it to you straight."

Master Morgan bent his head. "Could you perchance use the little one for trading?" he inquired, his voice toneless.

"Who, me?" Hawkes laughed, a loud laugh. "Why, I'd sooner buy that weathervane horse on yonder barn! No, m'friend, I ain't buying one *or* t'other."

Little Bub opened wide his jaws, bared his teeth, and sneezed in Hiram Hawkes' face. Even Ebenezer laid back his ears.

"By ginger!" thought Joel. "Eb and Bub be good judges, too!" And he laughed softly in relief and happiness.

Pa Gets an Idea

THE SUN was almost overhead when Joel spied the sugar maples shading his own log house, and the sheep browsing in his front yard.

A quick, small cry escaped him, and he slipped between Ebenezer and Little Bub, trying to hold on to each. "Pa's heard the news!" he told himself as he turned in the gate. "Else why is he blocking the door, his feet planted solid like the ram's when he's fixing to butt?"

The next thing Joel knew, a slight figure had

darted around his father and was running down the path. "Joel boy!" a gentle voice was calling.

"We're home, Ma!"

His mother did not need to be told. Her eyes were flooded with happiness. She held the boy close and felt of him to make sure he was all in one piece. Then, quite satisfied, she shook Master Morgan's hand and went directly to Little Bub.

"He's little . . . and he's big, all to once!" she said, holding his face in the cup of her hands. "Like a little wood carving I used to have as a girl. And the other colt is real nice, too," she added quickly, as if Ebenezer had shown he was slighted. "Welcome home! All four of you." Suddenly remembering Mister Goss, she cast a worried glance in his direction.

He had not moved from the doorway. He stood rigid and stern, like a steersman at his post. Only a disrespectful breeze played with his brown beard.

"What can I do!" Joel thought desperately. "I got to make Pa see how smart the colts are." He stepped Ebenezer around, trying to show how well he led. His father's face did not change. Next, Joel put his bundle on Little Bub's back. Then he picked up the creature's feet, one at a time, as he had seen Farmer Beane do.

Grudgingly Mister Goss said, "Howdy." But he did not smile or nod. He ignored the colts completely.

"Maybe if they are looking out the door of our own shed," Joel thought, "maybe then they would seem part of the place and Pa would like them." He led Ebenezer away and whistled for Bub to come along.

The shed had not been used in a year, but Joel remembered that up in the loft there was still some timothy hay. He put the colts each in a stall and hurried up to the loft. He smelled of the timothy. It was not stale at all. He filled each manger. Then he scrubbed and filled the water buckets. As the colts began munching the hay and making themselves at home, Joel wished his father would come out to see how happy they were. With a sigh, he shuffled slowly toward the house.

"I repeat, sir, 'twas my doing, bringing the colts home," Justin Morgan was saying as Joel entered the kitchen. "I calculate to sell them." Then tiredly he started up the ladder to his room in the garret. "The fatigues of the journey have overcome me," he said over his shoulder. "Slumber is the best cure." And he closed the trap door behind him.

Mister Goss's eyes were blazing now. "Joel!" he bellowed. "The schoolmaster can talk till he's blue in the face, but I know 'twas you had a finger in this. And I don't aim to play nursemaid to two colts. Hear? I'm through having horses on the place." He turned to Mistress Goss now. "You recollect the last 'un? No sooner do I have him broke than he gets the strangles and I got to shoot him. What in tunket they think I am? They'll lark off to school and leave me to muck out and do their work. By thunder!" he exploded, pounding his fist on the table until the dishes jumped. "I won't have it!"

"Now don't get your dander up, Pa," soothed Mistress Goss, wondering if a piece of her fresh pumpkin pie would calm him. She brought the pie to the table and began marking it off into four big wedges.

Joe's father noticed the four wedges of pie, when there were only three people in the room. "And that ain't all!" he sputtered. "Boarding the schoolmaster's got to stop, too. High time he found a new place. Feeding four is costly." He stopped for breath, then added, "And 'tis high time our Joel learnt a trade."

Suddenly Mister Goss looked at Joel, measuring him with his eye. He stopped bellowing and now his voice wheedled, trying to persuade his wife. "The trip hardened the boy, Emma. Lookit his muscles beginning to show underneath his shirtsleeves."

Joel broke in softly. "Pa? Couldn't I just stay to home and take care of the colts and . . ."

"Lemme see now," Joel's father was thinking aloud. "Why, o' course, that's who 'twas."

"Who was who?" Mistress Goss asked timidly.

"Why, Mister Chase, o' course. I hearn he needs an apprentice boy to work part time at his mill and part time at his inn. Joel here's just the one for the job. Why, mostly all Joel's friends has been bound out a'ready."

The knife in the mother's hand dropped to the table with a clatter. "It doesn't do to act sudden about sending a boy away," she said, trying to keep fear out of her voice.

Joel felt like crying out, "I belong here. And the colts . . . they need *me.*" But the words died inside him.

" 'Tain't sudden at all," Mister Goss snorted. "Why, we got all the rest of the day to be mulling on it. In the morning me and Joel will call on Miller Chase. And now, Ma, I can do with a piece of that pie and a tankard of buttermilk."

To please his mother, Joel tried to eat, too. But even his favorite pumpkin pie was flannel in his mouth. Every spoonful stuck in his throat, like the time he had the quinsy. Unable to keep back the hot tears, he ran out of the house and let them fall into Little Bub's mane.

When his sobbing had quieted, he set to work with a new fierceness. He curried both colts and he dumped the water out of the buckets and ran to the spring pipe, letting them fill up again with clear, cold water. He cleaned out the shed, and bedded the stalls with wild grass that had already turned dry and golden.

Dimly he heard his father's voice, and several times he heard the kitchen door creaking on its hinges as someone came or went, but he was intent on his work. At suppertime, his mother called and he had to go in. One look at his father told the boy that matters had been settled. He ate in silence, and was glad for bedtime.

As he climbed the ladder steps, candle in hand, the schoolmaster called him into his small garret room. Spread out on the feather bed were the goose-quill pens, the silver inkhorn, the shiny hourglass, the brass candle snuffer — all the treasures which had made the room seem beautiful to Joel.

The schoolmaster cleared a space for the boy to sit down. Then he went on with his packing, talking as he worked. "Two heartening things happened to me this afternoon," he said. "I went to see the Jenks family up the road, and they agreed to board me. And, secondly, I found an honest horse dealer."

"You hain't!" cried Joel in alarm.

"Joel! I thought you were all over saying 'hain't'!"

"But the little colt — he's not sold?"

The schoolmaster laughed. "I've a good home for Ebenezer, but news of Little Bub has traveled like wildfire. 'Too small! Too small!' everyone says. 'And besides, he isn't broken, to saddle *or* harness!'"

Joel leaned forward eagerly. He thought he could guess what the schoolmaster had in mind.

"Now, Joel, what I ask of you is this — "

"Yes?"

"Do you think you could gentle Little Bub?"

Could he gentle Little Bub? Had he thought of anything else, awake or asleep? " 'Course I could!" he said, his eyes shiny. "I been watching Pa gentle colts ever since I was a baby."

Then suddenly all the eagerness faded. "You mean . . ." He broke off the drippings of the candle and nervously formed them into a ball. "You mean I'm to gentle him — for someone else?"

"That's what I really mean, lad. We are both more fond of Little Bub than men should be of any beast; but I have debts to pay, and I must pay them before I die. I need your help, Joel. Will you shake hands, man to man?"

The boy hesitated a long moment. Then, taking a deep breath, he put his hand into the thin, dry one of the schoolmaster.

"Thank you, Joel. Now then," the master continued in a more cheerful tone, "if Miller Chase takes you on, he will be obliged to send you to night school. I wonder," he said, wrapping a faded waistcoat about his reading boards and songbooks, "I wonder if you wouldn't like to spend an hour with the colt after lessons each night."

"In the dark?"

Justin Morgan snuffed out his own tallow candle, and then Joel's. He threw wide the shutters and drew the boy to the gable window. The moon was three-quarters full. It sifted through the trees and spattered the yard with a magical white light.

"For two weeks," he said, "there will be light enough for *you* to see. Horses, you know, can see quite well in the dark."

Seven Years! Seven Years!

THE NEXT MORNING Joel's mother set down a big platter of fried ham and oatcakes in front of him, as if already he were a visitor instead of family.

Joel smiled up at her. "I feel like Preacher Clapsaddle," he said, "come to pay a call."

"See that you stow away your food like Preacher Clapsaddle!" his mother replied, with a catch in her voice.

Then they both laughed at the remembrance of

the preacher eating so heartily that he kept tucking his beard into his mouth along with the food, and had to pull it out again and pat it dry.

"How nice it is," Joel thought, "that Ma and I can laugh even when we feel all pinched up inside."

Mister Goss clumped in then, and breakfast became a business to be finished with dispatch. "Sniggering and tomfoolery have small place in this workaday world," he said, shaking a forefinger. "Won't be no such nonsense at Miller Chase's, I kin promise you that!"

The meal was eaten in silence, with only the sounds of chewing and swallowing and Mister Goss's pewter cup brought down sharply on the table.

At last the father wiped his mouth and stood up to go. He motioned to Joel to follow, and without a word the man and the boy marched out into the morning sunshine and set off for Chase's Inn.

Only once did Joel turn back. His mother, looking very small, was waving her apron at him, a white flag of courage.

It was almost a mile to Chase's Inn, and all the way Joel walked with head bent, letting dreams take over his thoughts. He made believe the colts were right behind him. Once he imagined he heard Ebenezer neighing and Little Bub sending forth his high notes which died out in that low rumble. He tried hard to listen, but Mister Goss was ranting on about the sorry condition of the Jenkses' fence, and Joel could not be sure.

As they passed the Jenkses' house, he hoped for a glimpse of the schoolmaster, but the only sign of life was a yellow hound pup sniffing along a hedgerow. Joel said to himself, "Little Bub hain't going to like that hound-dog, if what Farmer Beane told us was sure enough true."

As luck would have it, Thomas Chase was alone, working on his accounts, when Joel and his father walked into the office of the inn. He paused, quill pen in hand, and looked up from under his bushy eyebrows.

"Wal," he smiled, noting the worried look on Joel's face, "ain't nothing in the world so bad nor so good as it seems. Now what kin I do fer you two?"

Mister Goss wasted no time on pleasantries. He went right to the point. "I'd admire," he said, "to have you take on my Joel as your apprentice. With a sawmill and an inn to tend, you need a stout lad to help. Joel here will be handy as the pocket on your coat!"

The miller let his cool gray eyes travel over the boy with interest. Only this morning he had received a big order for barrel staves and hoops from the West Indies. Besides, Mistress Chase had been snappish of late. A likely lad — one who could buckle down to work — might make things easier all around.

"Hmmmm," he said, hedging for time. "It'll take a lusty lad to work by day and go to school by night, like the law requires."

Mister Goss thumped Joel on the back. "The boy ain't what you'd call a strapper — that is, not to look at — but he's tough as leather."

"Hmmmm!" the miller said again, trying to compare this boy with an overfat one who had come to see him just last evening. He put down his pen and looked earnestly at Joel.

"Y'know, son," he said, " 'twouldn't be no snap around here. There's an awful lot of hand sawing to do, and Mistress Chase is mighty smart at thinkin' up chores. A boy'd have to be strong as a bear and quick as a cat."

"Show him your muscle, son. Make a fist and show him."

Joel winced. His eye fell on the wall clock behind Mister Chase. The hour hand pointed exactly to seven. Below the dial the pendulum was hidden in a glass case painted with flying white doves, and the words, "Time is fleeting."

Joel obeyed his father. What did it matter if Miller Chase laughed at his puny arm? In a few seconds it would be all over. He made his fist and flexed his muscle, while his mind repeated the words, *Time is fleeting, time is fleeting, time is . . .*"

At last he brought his gaze away from the clock. To his surprise, the miller was not laughing. His

49

gray eyes were filled with kindness. "Boy," he said, "I recollect when I was a youngling with no more muscle than you got. But I was full o' spunk, and for a word o' encouragement I could do a man's lick of work."

Joel smiled in relief. He heard his father cough hesitantly, then heard his voice come, oily nice. "Uh . . . Chase . . . uh . . . ah . . . stands to reason Joel could saw a bit o' lumber for my use if'n it didn't interfere with his regular labors?"

Mister Chase was listening with only half his mind. Suddenly he wanted this boy. He had always hoped for a son of his own and there was something about Joel, not just the gangly growing look, but something about the eyes that he liked. A kind of awareness, like a startled deer. Yet there was trust in them, too. Yes, here was a lad he would be proud to look upon as his own. "If the boy be willing," he said slowly, thoughtfully, "it would very well suit me to take him."

"Ahem . . . Chase . . . and about that free lumber?"

The miller waved his hand impatiently. "Yes to that, too. Now let's step over to the Justice of the Peace and have him draw up the papers all proper-like."

"What papers?" a high, sharp voice demanded. It belonged to Mistress Chase, who swept into the room wearing a red wrapper and a scowl that said,
50

"Ain't nothing goin' to happen around here without *my* say-so."

Thomas Chase turned around. "This boy," he explained to his wife, "is ready to be parceled out. He'll be considerable help to both of us."

To the man's amazement, his wife nodded vigorously, and the white flounces on her cap went up and down like waves billowing. "Aye!" she agreed. "The skinny ones be quicker."

All this while the big hand on the clock had moved but five minutes. Joel swallowed hard. In five minutes he had lived a whole lifetime! In five minutes he had grown from boy to man.

Woodenly he followed along after his father and the miller as they walked through the public room of the inn and out of doors and down the road to the small weathered house of the Justice of the Peace.

The office of the Justice was a crowded-in place — the desk too big for the room, and the chairs set at awkward angles, so that Joel stumbled over one and almost fell flat. There was a clock here, too, a big one, very plain, without doves or cupids or words of wisdom. Its tick was loud and doleful as it tolled the seconds.

The Justice, a black-frocked spider of a man, listened to Mister Chase's story and began at once to fill in the blank spaces on a printed sheet. After some time he peered over his spectacles at Joel and said in a whiny voice, "Boy! Repeat after me: I, Joel Goss . . ."

"*I, Joel Goss . . .*" came the frightened voice.

The whine went on, ". . . of my own free will, and by the consent of my father . . ."

"*Of my own free will, and by the consent of my father . . .*"

"Doth put myself apprentice to . . ."

"*Doth put myself apprentice to . . .*"

"Thomas Chase of Randolph, Innkeeper and Miller . . ."

Joel turned white. He felt as if his whole body were going through the sawmill, being ground into bits. He grabbed at his father's sleeve. But Mister Goss stood straight and unmoving, as if no more than a fly had lit on him. A sob meant to be a silent one escaped the boy as he repeated:

"*Thomas Chase of Randolph, Innkeeper and Miller . . .*"

The voice of the Justice twanged on: ". . . until the full term of seven years be compleat and ended."

"Seven years!" Joel cried. And "*Seven years! Seven years!*" the clock tolled. The boy stared at the clock. Things were happening to him. Without a hand touching him, he was being shoved down the years.

"During the aforesaid term," the Justice was saying, "I, Joel Goss . . ."

"During the aforesaid term, I, Joel Goss . . ."

"Shall never absent myself day or night without leave . . ."

Joel imagined he saw his mother's face now, wiping away a tear. He saw her crying into Little Bub's mane, just as he had done. His words came without his willing them.

"Shall never absent myself day or night without leave . . ."

"But shall always . . ."

"But shall always . . ."

"Obey my master's commands . . ."

"Obey my master's commands . . ."

"And keep his secrets."

"And keep his secrets."

The Justice stopped to scratch his ear with the goose-quill pen. Then he quickened his pace and went on without pausing now for Joel. "Said master shall teach said apprentice the art or mystery of a sawyer, and shall provide for him sufficient meat, drink, apparel, lodging, and washing befitting an apprentice, and shall send him to school every winter at night."

He took a deep breath, then plunged rapidly on, chanting the familiar words until they ran together without meaning. "At the completion of said term, the master shall provide for the apprentice one new suit of apparel, four shirts, and two neckletts.

"In witness whereof Philip Goss, Thomas Chase,

53

and Joel Goss have put their hands and seals this twenty-fifth day of September, one thousand seven hundred and ninety-five."

A spidery hand held out the goose-quill pen to Joel. And the whiny voice said, "Now, boy, sign here, in the presence of your father and Thomas Chase and before me, Jacobus Spinks, Justice of the Peace for the village of Randolph in the County of Orange in the State of Vermont."

"*Sign here!*" ticked the clock. "*Sign here! Sign here!*"

Again Joel turned to his father, eyes imploring: "Do I have to, Pa?"

But again there was no answer. Mister Goss's arms were folded across his chest and his gaze held to a fixed spot on the ceiling.

At last Joel picked up the pen and curved his thumb and fingers about it. He sat down on the chair that the miller pulled up for him, and put his arm on the desk. His eye followed the black-nailed finger pointing to a dotted line.

"Yes, Mister Spinks," he murmured, "I see the place you mean." And with trembling hand he wrote in his round childish scrawl:

Joel Goss

A Stranger Knocking

YESTERDAY, today, tomorrow — all the same. Get up before dawn. Tiptoe down the ladder steps. Feed the fire. Sweep the hearth. Eat a dry oatcake. Head for the mill. Sweep up yesterday's sawdust. Saw clapboards by hand. Saw pipe-staves. Eat sawdust. Breathe sawdust. Sawdust in your hair, your ears, your boots. Saw! Saw until your muscles ache!

Yesterday, today, tomorrow dragging by, dragging by. Only the nighttimes different. The chores all done and supper eaten. And now the seeming miracle — now the nighttimes belonging to Joel.

He was free then to go to evening school, where he read and wrote and ciphered and sang. He sang until his lungs were fit to burst, as if the louder he sang, the sooner his big happiness would come.

Then the moment Master Morgan dismissed class, Joel flew out the door and ran to the Jenks place — past the house, past the woodpile, past the chicken coops, leaping across the root cellar, to the shed behind the house.

Suddenly all the tiredness washed out of the boy, and a sharp ecstasy filled him. There was Little Bub waiting for *him*, waiting to hear his name called out, waiting to scratch his head up and down Joel's rough jacket.

"Feller," Joel would gasp, out of breath. "I been waitin', too!"

The colt's quizzical face butted Joel. Then he stamped and pawed with a forefoot. "Let's *do* something!" he seemed to say.

Never was a creature more willing to be gentled. After but two lessons, he wore a halter as if it were part of him. Like his forelock. Or his tail. Fastening two ropes to the halter, Joel drove him around and around in a circle, teaching him to "git up" and to "whoa."

Next Joel slipped a bit in the colt's mouth. At first Bub's ears went back in displeasure. He did not mind rope or leather things, but iron felt cold and hard to his tongue. One night Joel warmed the bit in his hands and coated it with maple syrup. From then on Little Bub accepted it each time, actually reaching out for it, jaws open wide.

Whenever the colt learned a new lesson, Joel told him what a fine, smart fellow he was. "Soon you'll be *big* for your size!" he would say. "And then you've got to be so smart and willing that even an ornery man won't have reason to whop ye. I couldn't abide that!" he added in dread.

Some nights Joel fastened a lantern to an old two-wheeled cart borrowed from Mister Jenks. Then, filling the cart with stones for weight, he drove Bub

over the rolling hills. He practiced pulling him up short. He practiced walking him, trotting him, stopping and backing him.

The moon waned and became full again. By now Joel was galloping Little Bub, galloping him bareback across the fields. And Bub wanted to go! It was as if the clean, cold air felt good in his lungs, as if he liked the night and the wind and the boy.

One evening when Master Morgan remained late at school, Joel burst in on him so full of laughter he could scarcely talk. The other apprentice boys had gone long ago, and Joel's laughter rang out so heartily in the empty room that the schoolmaster joined in without knowing why.

Between spasms the boy managed to gasp, "You should've seed that little hound-dog run!"

"What little hound-dog?"

"Why, Mister Jenks's yellow one," giggled Joel, bursting into fresh laughter. "He come a-tearin' out the house, yammering at Little Bub, tryin' to nip his legs. Oh, ho, ho, ho!"

"What did Bub do?"

"What did he *do*?" shrieked Joel. "Why, he sprung forward like a cat outen a bag. And that idiot hound was too addled to go home. He streaked down the road with Bub after him."

Joel had to wipe away his tears before he could go on. "By and by," he chuckled, "the hound got so beat out I took pity on him and reined in."

Master Morgan's eyes twinkled. "I reckon Farmer Beane was right," he said. "Seems as if Little Bub and dogs just don't cotton to each other."

When Mister Goss first heard that Joel was training the schoolmaster's colt, he was furious. But later, when neighbors marveled at the boy's skill, he boasted and bragged about it: "All that boy knows about horses he got from me!"

The truth of the matter was that in watching his father train a colt Joel had learned what not to do, as well as what to do. While his father could break and train in a matter of hours, his horses often seemed broken in spirit, too. The boy was determined that this should not happen to his colt. And it had not. Little Bub's eyes were still dancy. He still tossed his mane and nosed the sky. He still had a frisky look about him. No, he had lost none of his spirit.

Even in the rough winds of winter, the colt's schooling went right on, night after night. And about the time when Joel began to think Little Bub might be his forever, a stranger came knocking at the schoolhouse door.

School was in full session. A dozen apprentice boys were bent over their copybooks. As if on one stem, a dozen heads turned around.

Master Morgan pushed his spectacles up on his forehead, brushed the chalk off his vest, and went to the door. "Come in, sir," he said.

A tall, gaunt man entered and sat down on the splint-bottomed chair which the schoolmaster offered. "Good evening," he said a voice that rolled out strong. "I'm Ezra Fisk, a new settler, and word has come to my ear that you have a horse to rent."

Eleven pens stopped scratching and eleven pairs of eyes looked up with interest. Joel's pen skated wildly across the page as if his arm had been jolted out of its socket.

"You will continue with your work," the schoolmaster nodded to the boys. He could not bring himself to answer the man's question at once.

Mister Fisk filled in the silence that followed. "I've been watching a lad ride a smallish horse in the moonlight," he said in his trumpet of a voice, "and by inquiring at the inn, I understand the horse belongs to you, sir."

Justin Morgan made a steeple out of his fingers. His "yes" was spoken through tight lips.

"You see," the newcomer explained, "I have a piece of wooded land along the White River. And Robert Evans, my hired hand, will need a horse to help clear it. This fellow, Evans, is a brawny man, and I figure he and a horse with some get-up-and-git could clear the land in a year's time."

Master Morgan hesitated a long moment before he spoke. "You would like to buy the horse, sir?"

"Tsk, tsk, Morgan. No, indeed! Who would buy

such a *little* animal? As I said, I merely wish to rent him."

The schoolmaster stood up and looked questioningly at Joel. Ezra Fisk followed his glance. "That the boy who's been riding the colt?"

"Aye," Master Morgan said very softly. "And for his sake I am loathe to part with the animal."

The visitor now lowered his voice, too. "I understand," he said, leaning one arm on the desk, "that you are paid sometimes in Indian corn and sometimes the full sum of two dollars per week. Yet even the latter amount," he added knowingly, "covers no such extras as horses and harpsichords."

Joel sat forward, holding his breath, trying to hear the next words.

"But I, my good man," and now the voice waxed strong again, "stand ready to pay fifteen dollars a year, and the animal's keep, of course."

He said no more.

The noise of the scratching pens faded away. A stray flutter of smoke went up the chimney with a faint hiss. Joel was afraid he was going to cry. He wanted to run to Little Bub and hide him away somewhere deep in the woods. Perhaps this was all a bad dream. It *must* be a bad dream! Why else would his head drop forward in a nod, answering "yes" to the schoolmaster's unspoken question?

The next afternoon Joel was setting a log in the

sawmill when he heard the creaking of a wagon wheel and the cloppety-clop of hoofs coming down the road. This in itself was nothing to make him stop work, but from the uneven beat of the hoofs he could tell that the animals were not traveling in a team. And then, without looking up, he knew. He knew that the lighter hoofbeats were those of Little Bub. He started the saw, and then he turned and faced the road.

It *was* Little Bub, all right, not five rods away. He was tied to the back of a wagon pulled by a team of oxen. His reddish coat glinted in the sunlight, and he held his head high, as if he found nothing at all disgraceful in being tied to an oxcart.

The blood hammered in Joel's head. He might have called out, "Hi, Little Bub!" and felt the hot pride of having him nicker in reply. Instead, he kept hearing the schoolmaster's words: "I've got to pay off my debts before I die. Will you gentle the colt for me, lad?"

Well, Bub had been gentled, all right. Anyone could see that. With a heavy heart, Joel watched the procession as it passed him by, and then clattered over the log bridge and climbed up and up the steep hill. At last it disappeared over the brow, and nothing was left of it. Nothing but a wisp of dust.

The Pulling Bee

In the weeks that followed, it was hard for Joel to pay attention to his work. He kept seeing Little Bub in the back of his mind, seeing him go lickety-split after the hound-dog, or just capering for the fun of it. And in the sound of the millwheel he kept hearing the high, bugling neigh. And often, when no one was looking, he would sniff his jacket to smell the very essence of Little Bub!

In whatever Joel was doing — gathering stones for fences, wielding a mattock on stumps in the highway, working inside or outside — the little horse nudged into his thoughts.

One day, when Joel was up inside the chimney sweeping away the soot, his ears picked out three names from the talk going on in the room below: Ezra Fisk, Robert Evans, Justin Morgan. Precariously his fingers clung to the bricks like a bird. If he made the least noise or if his bare feet slid into view, the talk might stop or take a new tack altogether. His toes found a narrow ledge of brick and caught a foothold. His whole body tensed with listening.

"Yup," a voice was saying, "the schoolmaster's little horse is turning out to be a crack puller. Already he's made a nice clearing of about five acres."

Another voice said, "So the little horse can pull, eh?"

"Yup," the first voice replied. "Evans brags that the critter can jerk a log right out of its bark!"

A loud guffaw greeted the remark.

In the dark of the chimney Joel smiled in pride. But what if — the smile faded, and worry crept in — what if Evans was working Little Bub too hard? What if he became swaybacked and old before his time?

Joel had to know. Quickly he slid down the chimney and dropped to the hearth. But he was too late. All he saw was the whisk of a coattail and the door to the public room swinging shut, and at the same time Mistress Chase coming at him with a broken lock to be mended.

As the days went by, Joel heard more and more about Little Bub's labors, and his worry sharpened. At last he talked things over with Miller Chase.

"Why, work don't hurt horses," Mister Chase said reassuringly. "It's t'other way around. Idleness is what really hurts 'em. Their muscles git soft and their lungs git so small they can't even run without wheezing."

And so Joel's mind was eased.

By the time spring came on, Joel and the miller were the best of friends. In the late afternoon while Mistress Chase napped, he often waved Joel away with a smile. "Be off with you now. Have a mite of fun," he would say.

Joel took delight in these free afternoon hours. At this time of day Chase's Mill was the liveliest spot on the White River. Farmers would congregate to chat as they waited for the big saw to cut their logs. And often they tested the strength of their horses with a log-pulling contest. Surely, Joel thought, Little Bub must show up some day.

It was on a late afternoon in April that his hopes were realized. The millstream had grown swollen with spring rains, and Mister Chase had taken on a helper to keep the mill sawing logs both night and day.

On this afternoon, when the yard was crowded

with farmers, the miller called to Joel. "See the man studying that there pine log? That's Nathan Nye. And if Nathan Nye is about, acting mighty important and bossy, you can be expecting most anything to happen. He was ever good at fixing pulling contests."

Joel watched the jerky-legged man hop from one group to another, like a puppet on a string.

"If I was a boy, now, with no chores to do," the miller smiled, "it seems like I'd skedaddle right out there and be in the center of things."

In no time at all Joel was helping Mister Nye wrap tug chains about the huge pine log. A big dappled mare stood waiting to have the chains hooked to her harness.

The mare's owner, Abel Hooper from Buttonwood Flats, was too busy bragging to be of any help. "A mighty lucky thing I'm first," he was saying. "Big Lucy and me'll pull this here piece o' kindling onto the logway in one pull. Then you can all hyper on home afore lantern time."

Abel Hooper had to eat his words. Big Lucy tried hard. She dug her forefeet into the earth and tugged and tugged, but the log barely trembled. Even when he poked her with the prodding stick, she only looked around as if to tell him it was useless.

One after another the work horses had their turn. Yet no matter how whips cracked or masters yelled, the log seemed rooted to earth.

Nathan Nye made a megaphone of his hands. "Folks!" he shouted. "Guess it's just too hefty for a horse. You men with oxen can have a try now."

Just then a bearded farmer came riding up on a chunky young stallion. Joel's heart missed a beat. Could this be Little Bub? This unkempt, mud-coated horse? Why, small as he was, he looked to be a six- or even a seven-year-old! Then Joel grinned as the little stallion let out a high bugle and a rumbling snort.

"Wait!" called the big man astride the little horse. "Here's a critter wants to try."

A smile, half scorn, half amusement, crossed Nathan Nye's face. "Evans," he said, "ye're crazy as if ye'd burnt yer shirt. Look at Big Lucy. She's still blowin' from the try. And Biggle's Belgian — his muscles are still a-hitchin' and a-twitchin'. Even Wiggins' beast failed. Can't none of 'em budge that log."

"None exceptin' my one-horse team!" crowed Evans.

Fear caught at Joel as a silence fell upon the crowd.

And then came the rain of words, mingled with laughter. "*That* little sample of a horse!"

"Why, his tail is long as a kite's!"

"Yeah, he's liable to get all tangled up and break a leg."

"Morgan's horse," Evans said slowly, "ain't exactly what you'd call a drafter, but whatever he's hitched to generally has to come."

Joel heard the sharp voice of Mistress Chase calling: "Boy! You come here!"

"Oh, rats!" he muttered under his breath. On the way to the inn he stopped long enough to put his cheek against Little Bub's. "I'll be back," he whispered. "I'll be right back."

Mistress Chase met him just inside the door with a kettle of hasty pudding. "Hang the kettle over the fire," she commanded, "and stir and stir until I tell you to quit."

He hung the kettle on the crane and set to work. "*Hasty* pudding!" Joel cried to himself. "It beats me how it got its name! Nothing quick about this!" Suddenly he heard the clump of boots and looked around to see Evans, followed by a little company of men, strut into the inn.

"Madam Innkeeper!" Evans called. "I'm wagering a barrel o' cider that my horse can move the pine log. But now, pour me a mugful. I'm dying of thirst."

Joel was stirring so vigorously he almost upset the pudding. Mistress Chase let out a shriek. "Boy! Mind what you're doing! Hasty pudding's not meant to feed the fire!"

For once he paid no heed. He tore across the room and grabbed Mister Evans by the sleeve. "Sir!"

he cried. "Little Bub's been working hard all day. Please don't ask him to pull that big log."

Evans gulped his drink. "Go 'way," he snapped in annoyance. "When I want advice, I'll not ask it of a whippersnapper. I know that horse!" He stomped out of doors, the others joking and laughing behind him.

While Joel stirred the pudding, he kept looking out the window. He could see Little Bub nibbling all the fresh green shoots within his range. And he could see the men sizing him up, feeling of his legs, then making their wagers.

One by one, the stars dusted the sky. Nathan Nye brought out a lantern so that Evans could see to fasten the tug chains to the log.

"I just *got* to go out there now!" Joel pleaded. "Ma'am, if you please, could I?"

Mistress Chase nodded. "You're stirring so strong that hasty pudding's heaving like a sea. Go on! Git out, afore ye upset it."

"Oh, thanks, ma'am," Joel murmured as he bolted for the door, vaulted over a barrel of cider, and ran to the mill, where Evans was stepping off ten rods.

"Aye, fellers!" he was saying. "Bub can do it — in two pulls." He turned around, almost stumbling over the boy. "A nettle hain't half as pesky as you," he growled. "Out of my way or I'll clout you!"

Nathan Nye shouted to Evans. "Mebbe you'd

oughter listen to the lad. Want to give up afore you start?"

"No such a thing! Why, I'm actually ashamed to ask Morgan's horse to pull a splinter like this. Now, if you'll find me three stout men to sit astride the log, why, then I'll ask him."

Joel ran to Little Bub. "Oh, my poor little feller," he choked. "None of the big critters could do it, and now with three men besides! Oh, Bub, Bub . . ."

Laughter was ringing up and down the valley. "Ho-ho-ho — that pint-sized cob to pull such a big log! Ho-ho . . ."

Nathan Nye had no trouble at all in finding three brawny volunteers. As the men straddled the log, they joked and laughed and poked one another in the ribs.

"Look to your feet, men!" warned Evans. "This horse means business. Something's got to give."

Nye held the lantern aloft. It lighted the huddle of faces. They were tense with excitement. Some of the men were placing last-minute bets. Some were chewing madly on wisps of hay. Others twirled their hats and wrung them nervously. Joel felt as if he were going to be sick.

Evans repeated his warning. "Look to your feet, men!"

Someone tittered.

Then the silence exploded as Evans roared, "Git up!"

The sharp word of command galvanized the little horse into action. His muscles swelled and grew firm. He backed ever so slightly. He lowered his head, doubling down into the harness. He lunged, half falling to his knees, straining forward, throwing his whole weight into the collar.

A hush closed around the gathering. It hung heavy and ominous. Suddenly the very earth seemed to shake. The chains were groaning, the log itself trembling as if it had come alive. It began to skid. It was moving! The stout man aboard laughed hysterically, then sobered, trying to balance himself, clutching onto the others. The log kept on moving. It was halfway to the mill!

The horse's breath whistled in his lungs. His nostrils flared red in exertion. Sweat broke out on his body, lathering at the collar and traces. Joel, too, was drenched in sweat. He was struggling, straining, panting as if he were yoked alongside Little Bub.

Now the terrible silence again as the horse stood to catch his wind. There was no sound at all from the crowd. Overhead a robin, trying to get settled for the night, chirped insistently.

Now Evans commanded again. And again the horse backed slightly, then snatched the log into motion. Again the log was sliding, sliding, sliding. This time it did not stop until it reached the saw-mill!

Still none of the onlookers made a sound. The three men astride were as silent as the log they sat upon. Only the horse's breathing pierced the quiet.

Then as if a dike had opened, there was a torrent of noise. Everyone began shouting at once. "Hooray for Little Bub! Hooray for Evans and Justin Morgan! Hooray for the big-little horse!"

Joel rushed over and threw his arms around Bub's neck. His whole body ached, as if he had moved the log himself. "It's over! It's over! You did it, Bub! You did it!" he kept repeating, sobbing a little from exhaustion and relief.

The horse lipped Joel's cheek and neck. He almost tried to say, "It's all right, boy; don't be taking it so hard." He was winded and leg-weary, but it was good to be near the boy again. It was good.

He nickered softly.

Stronger'n a Ox

AFTER THE log-pulling contest Joel saw the little horse more often. Nearly every week Bub was challenged, and except for the time Nathan Nye disqualified him for starting too quickly and breaking the log chains, he always won.

His fame as a strong puller grew, and men soon dropped the affectionate name of Little Bub. They spoke of him with respect: *"Morgan's horse* is handy, quick, and strong." *"Morgan's horse* can pull like living quicksand." Everywhere he became known as

73

"Morgan's horse," and his prowess spread up and down the valley.

The schoolmaster himself began taking a lively interest in his colt. Much as he disliked noisy gatherings and betting, he could not stay away from the pulling matches. "Farmer Beane's premium," he told Joel one day after cheering himself hoarse, "just can't be beat!"

Day by day the colt's muscles hardened, until at last Abel Hooper and the other farmers refused to enter their drafters and oxen in the pulling matches. " 'Tain't no use," they said. "The Morgan's stronger'n a ox."

Spring wore on, and another five acres of Mister Fisk's land was cleared and burned over and planted. All up and down the valley men were pushing the wilderness back, then striking their axes in the black earth and dropping kernels of Indian corn in the holes they made.

Mistress Chase had several acres of ground she called her own, and Joel was taken away from his work at the mill to seed it. He was told to bring his handspike along to dig the pockets for the kernels, but when he began covering them and tamping the earth with his boot, Mistress Chase went into a fury. "You get down on yer knees and press them seeds in with the heel of yer hand, not yer foot," she yelled as she stood over him. " 'Tain't hocus-pocus makes corn grow; it's out-and-out work."

74

To Joel the hours and the days of planting seemed never ending. Strike the earth with the handspike, drop in the kernels, press the earth. Strike, drop, press. Strike, drop, press. Twinges of pain shot through his legs, his back, his arms. Often at sundown he lay in the dirt and cried, hoping tomorrow would never come.

Grown men, too, were worn out with planting. Even hoeing-in wheat and rye and oats was slow, back-breaking work. When night came, they longed for excitement, for something to make them forget their weariness. They missed the pulling matches.

It was Nathan Nye who thought up quarter-mile racing. There was an open straightaway along one branch of the White River, quite free of trees. "I'll make it into the neatest racing strip this side of New York!" he promised the settlers. On his black gelding he went to call on every tradesman in Randolph — the saddler, the carpenter, the printer, the blacksmith, the wigmaker, and all the rest. He figured that if each one lent his apprentice boy for an hour a day, the raceway could soon be scraped as smooth as any track in the big cities.

Nathan Nye was a man who got what he wanted. He had a determination about him, and he knew how to put a question to get a Yes answer. "How-de-do," he would say, shaking hands with the tradesman. "Ezra Sneveley and Josh Cobb wanter loan

75

me their bound boys to fix up a strip for a little racing. How 'bout you?"

While the man tried to make up his mind, Nathan Nye pounded his fist on his hand. "Where'd you be without the farmer? And him workin' his insides out, making fields outa wilderness and crops outa fields. He needs a little fun at the tag end of day. Me and you got to lift his weariness."

The tradesman would bob his head up and down in agreement. Afterward he was never quite sure whether he had come to the decision on his own, or had just been swept along, the way a branch in a stream is swept along by the current.

It was tedious work, making a race track out of a rutted path, but the apprentice boys welcomed the change. They arrived on the scene whistling and laughing and swinging big iron kettles. Under Nathan Nye's direction, they turned the kettles upside down and dragged them back and forth, using the sharp rims as planes to level off the path.

Joel worked with a fierceness, scraping harder than the other boys, grubbing out every root with his bare fingers to be sure there were no knobs or snags. If Little Bub lost a race it would be no disgrace, but if he stumbled over a root and never got up again, then the disgrace and the hurt would be Joel's.

Nathan Nye watched over the work with a careful eye, scolding and encouraging the boys by turns.

Finally one day he stood by with a look of satisfaction on his face. "Well, boys, that about does 'er," he said. "Yes, that be a fair racing strip."

The day of the first race was bright and brisk. It was the kind of day that makes men and horses want to go. A strong wind was blowing down from the north. It got into the horses' nostrils, exciting them.

Mister Nye, who was both starter and timekeeper, argued for waiting. "We need more entries," he said. "We've only three — my own black gelding, and Nanny Luddy here, and Morgan's Bub. Why, our race course is wide enough for six, maybe seven, horses."

The other farmers were cagey and only shook their heads. They wanted to look on a time or two to see how fast was the pace and what horse they had to beat.

But if entries were few, spectators were many. All the tradesmen were there, with their apprentice boys who had scraped the track, and all the farmers from roundabout, and friendly Indians from the Pennakook and Caughnawaga tribes, and of course the schoolmaster and Joel.

Just before Mister Nye dropped his hat as the signal to go, Joel overheard the wigmaker say to the saddler, "The Morgan horse may be stronger'n a ox, but good pullers usually be slow runners. I'm betting on Nanny Luddy."

"Yeah," the saddler agreed, "when it comes to

running, a pulling horse is slow as a hog on ice with his tail froze in."

Joel bristled. He wanted to speak his mind, to tell the men how fast Little Bub could gallop. But the crowd was shouting, "Bring 'em on! Bring 'em on!"

The Morgan drew center position. He was full of life and spirit, and at the drop of the hat he shot to the front with such a rush that the mare and the gelding just followed along, like horses hitched in tandem. It was all over so quickly that Joel and the schoolmaster stood staring in open-mouthed wonder. Not until Judge Nye announced that the Morgan had run the quarter-mile in thirty-six seconds did they whoop and holler with the rest.

Then a voice spoke low. It was Joel's voice whis-

pering to himself. "I reckon he liked the track tol'-able well."

He made his way through the crowd to Little Bub, who was trying to nose the people aside so he could reach the leaves of a big white elm. Joel leaped into the air, caught and bent the twig within range of Bub's lips. "Yep, feller," he smiled, as he ran his dirt-grimed hand over the lathered neck, "you must've liked the track tol'able well!"

A Challenge from New York

ON PLEASANT EVENINGS now the cares and labors of the day were forgotten in the sport of racing. The most respected member of the community, the preacher, encouraged the fun by his mere presence. He knew that good fellowship made tomorrow's tasks easier for his hard-working flock.

Even Mistress Chase approved all the hullabaloo of the race matches. To her it meant the spectators would yell their throats dry, and a call for freshening tankards of cider, along with her famous caraway cakes.

As for Joel, he lived all the day for a sight of the Morgan horse, his Little Bub, flying down the track to victory.

The horse himself took the sport in stride, just as he took work. He set his own record for speed, then broke it and set a new one. He became the most talked-about horse in the whole countryside. "That Morgan stallion's a torpedo!" men said. "He's partner to the wind." " 'Tis the fastest goer in all Vermont." Wherever men gathered — around the cracker and pickle barrels at the general store, or at the inn, or in the churchyard after Sunday meeting — they wagged their heads and chuckled over the doings of the pint-sized stallion. His every characteristic was admired.

"Beats me how he bugles a tune when he neighs."

"Mebbe it's 'cause he belongs to the singin' master!"

Then the men would burst into hearty laughter, each one adding his own observation.

"Beats me how he abominates dawgs; it's like they all had the hydrophoby."

"Beats me how he disrelishes sorghum, but is sweet on maple sugar."

"Beats me how he can roll over, even on a uphill slant."

At last the talk flew beyond the state. One day the mail coach from Albany, New York, drew up to a stop in front of the old log schoolhouse. The driver, a smiling young fellow, jumped down and presented himself to the singing master, who came out to greet him.

"Be ye Justin Morgan?"

The schoolmaster nodded his Yes.

"A wealthy gentleman," the driver said, as he fished a letter from his boot, "give me this with sharp instruction to see you got it personal." With a flourish he held out the letter. It was sealed with a splotch of wax and stamped with an elaborate coat of arms, and it smelled strongly of leather and snuff.

The worry lines of Master Morgan's brow deepened as he accepted the letter. He did not open it at once, but stood with his hand on the door latch. He watched the messenger climb onto his box and the coach-and-four lurch down the lane like some hunchbacked bug.

From inside the schoolhouse came the deep voices of the older boys and the high chatter of the girls. The schoolmaster turned now and went in. A hush fell over the room as he said, "You are dismissed for the day." He closed his songbook, put the pitch pipe away in the drawer of his desk, and began looking for his spectacles.

One of the pupils laughed on his way out. "They're on your head," he said, pointing. Then he sobered as he saw the master's frown.

Some of the children were eager to leave, wanting to run and catch the mail coach; and some shuffled out slowly, curious to learn what the letter held. Master Morgan hurried the slow ones along. He had not received a letter since his sister Eunice's husband had died, and if this one brought bad news, too, he wanted to be alone to read it.

In the silence of the empty schoolroom he slid a penknife under the seal and with trembling fingers unfolded the fine white paper. The handwriting, too, was fine, feather-fine. He pulled his spectacles down from his forehead, but even then he had to step to the light of the window and bring the letter up close. Sniffing again the odors of leather and snuff, he at last forced himself to read the words.

September 30, 1796
New York

Dear Sir:
It has come to my ears, through my erstwhile friend, Ezra Fisk, that the beast rented by him is owned by you. He also informs me that in spite of the scrubby size of said animal, it has some ability to run.

Now it so happens that my partner (the Honour-

able James Montague, Esquire) & I have business to attend in Brookfield, Vermont, a fortnight hence. We are the proud possessors of two elegant Thorough-breds known as Silvertail and Sweepstakes. For stamina & speed, for form & symmetry, they are not surpassed by any creature, either in Europe (where they were bred) or in America.

Hence what we propose is this: We challenge your work horse to run against our celebrated racers. The purpose being not for divertisement (amusement) but to prove, for once & all, the superiority of the Thorough-bred as against the mongrel-bred.

My partner & I know of the paltry salaries paid to schoolmasters (some, we hear, receiving but sixty-seven cents per week). Therefore, you will owe us nothing if your beast lose. Should he win, howsomever, we stand ready to pay to you the full purse of fifty dollars.

As our jockeys are hefty men, we stipulate that Fisk's hired man act as jockey for your beast, and not any flyweight boy.

For your edification, there is a beaver pond just beyond the Green Dragon Inn at Brookfield. A race course has been built around this pond, & I understand it measures a half mile & provides footing as good as may be expected in your backwoods country.

In fine, unless we hear from you to the contrary,

let us meet with our horses at the Green Dragon Inn, Brookfield, on the fifteenth day of October at the hour of five.

I have the honour to be, et cetera,

Master Morgan's face turned dark red in anger. With a show of vehemence, he creased the letter in its original folds and thrust it into the tail of his coat. The words scoured his mind. "Your *mongrel-bred!*" "Our *elegant Thorough-breds!*" "Your *work horse!*" "Our *celebrated racers!*"

Of a sudden Master Morgan's world was all action. He hurried outside, locked the schoolhouse door, and began running down the lane toward the village. He heard the letter crackle as his coattails floated and flapped in the wind, and it made him run all the faster. Halfway there, he overtook Mister Jenks driving his ox team.

"Justin! What's wrong?" Mister Jenks's voice was full of concern as he noted the flushed face of the schoolmaster.

"I'm all right. Just riled."

"You had me scairt, man. I swear I thought the schoolhouse was afire or the hull class murdered by Injuns. Climb aboard! Me and Nip and Tuck'll take you wherever 'twas you was goin'."

It struck the schoolmaster that whenever he needed help in a hurry, God sent Mister Jenks. He smiled now at the sunburnt face with its white lashes and brows. "If it please you, Jenks, would you be so kind as to drop me off at Ezra Fisk's house in Randolph? And whilst we're jogging along, I've an epistle to read you . . . soon as I catch my wind."

Ezra Fisk lived in a comfortable, rented cottage while he waited for his land to be cleared and his own house to be built. When the schoolmaster arrived, the family was seated at the table, eating cold gander and hot bread.

Mistress Fisk quickly set a place for the unexpected guest and nudged her boys to move closer together on their bench to make room for the schoolmaster.

"Have a thigh or a nice breast of gander," Mister Fisk urged heartily. "Time enough then to unburden your mind."

Smiling his thanks, the schoolmaster helped himself. He tried to pick at his food, but he was too excited to eat. Suddenly he could pretend no longer. He got up, reached inside his coattail, and presented the letter to Ezra Fisk. Then he sat down again, while every eye around the table focused on the letter. Master Morgan bent his head over his plate, his mind busy with questions. Would Mister Fisk be willing to race Little Bub? Would he let the horse and Evans, too, stop work for nearly a whole day? Could he spare them?

The face of the tall man was a mask as he read, now pursing his lips thoughtfully, now thinning them into a line. He read the letter once, and then to everyone's dismay began all over again. When he had finished his second reading, he folded and refolded the single sheet of paper, ran his finger over the gold seal, sniffed of the mingled odors, and returned the letter to Master Morgan.

At last his voice rolled out strong. "All right! All right, Morgan! They've asked for a whopping and we're going to give it to 'em!"

"Who, Pa? Who wants a whopping?" cried the older boy.

"Hush, son," said his mother.

Ezra Fisk picked up the bare drumstick from his plate and brandished it like a club. "Egad!" he trumpeted. "We'll give these New York gentry a royal run for their money. By all means, man, let us accept the challenge! I shall be more than glad to spare Evans and the horse — for a full half day," he added.

He signaled now to the schoolmaster to try to

eat, and he himself nibbled the gristle at the joint of a drumstick to show how good it was. Then, "Morgan!" he boasted, thumping himself on the chest. "When I rented your little cob, it appears I knew a thing or two about horseflesh. Eh?"

High-duck Dandies

News of the coming race traveled like forked lightning. The *Gazette* in Brookfield and the *Journal* in Randolph planned to run a full account of the event. Already they were setting type on the now-famous letter, and saving space for the story.

Meanwhile, everyone wanted to help the little Morgan get ready for the big day. It was Joel who asked the important question. "How do they start the horses in big races?" he inquired of Nathan

Nye. "Do they just drop a hat, the way you do?"

Mister Nye hemmed and hawed. He was unwilling to admit he had never been to a match where Thoroughbreds ran. Secretly he went around to Mister Fisk's house and there learned that sometimes a race was started by blast of trumpet or tap of drum, and sometimes a gong rang; but most often a pistol was raised, aimed, and fired — and the horses took off.

Accordingly, Mister Nye acquired a trumpet, a drum, a gong, and a pistol. Then in practice matches he let Joel act as jockey, and he used a different signal each time so that Little Bub would be familiar with them all.

Another thing Nathan Nye did. Instead of the usual quarter-mile race, he made Little Bub turn and run both ways of the track in order to build up to half-mile stamina.

A week before the big race, one of the farmers suggested clipping the Morgan's coat and trimming his fetlocks and chin whiskers, and even the hairs in his ears, to make him look stylish. But Master Morgan shook his head. "Often the nights be cold," he said. "Were the creature to take chills and ague, his wind would suffer."

And so Little Bub kept his shaggy coat, and he continued to work hard every day until the very hour when Evans rode him to Brookfield.

That day of the race, October 15, 1796, dawned fine and clear. Within a dozen miles of Brookfield everyone — goldsmiths, blacksmiths, barber-surgeons, wigmakers, clockmakers, hatters — made all sorts of excuses to close shop. Master Morgan dismissed school at noon. And Miller Chase, in a burst of generosity, let Joel take the afternoon off.

The boy had never been so excited. The sky was deep and blue, and the clouds had wings to them. He himself felt like some winged creature, having just escaped a dark old cocoon. He raced to the Jenkses' house, carrying a shabby satchel with holes in the corners where mice had been at work. While Mister Jenks was yoking Nip and Tuck, Joel did a little reconnoitering. Then, with laughter inside him, he climbed into the oxcart and settled himself between Mister Jenks and the schoolmaster.

"Seems good to be skylarking again, eh, Joel?" Master Morgan said as the wagon wheels whined and the oxen slow-footed ahead. "But why in the world did you bring a satchel? We'll be back before midnight, you know."

Joel grinned sheepishly. He turned around, pushing the bag toward the rear of the cart. "It's a surprise," he said, a mischief look in his eye.

The trip to Brookfield was uneventful. Up over one ridge and down again, with hills tumbling away to distance, and streams winding close.

"Barrin' a broken axle," Mister Jenks remarked, "we ought to be there a spell afore the others."

But when they entered the public room of the Green Dragon Inn, already there was a great bustle and stir. Tobacco smoke lay heavy on the air. It made Joel's eyes smart, and it set the schoolmaster to coughing.

Opposite the door and underneath the clock a little ticket counter had been set up. Men with silver dollars jingling in their hands were clustered about it, making their wagers. Joel sidled up to the line, and as he listened, the fun inside him was shot through by little arrows of fear. Nearly everyone who came in after looking at Silvertail and Sweepstakes bet *against* Little Bub.

Flushing in anger, Joel ran out to the stables behind the inn. Past sheds and troughs and wagons and horses he ran, his voice full of torment, crying: "They can't hold a candle to Bub. They can't! They can't!"

There were stalls for some forty horses in the stable, but only two were hidden by throngs of people. Joel joined the nearest line and made his way forward, borne by the surge of the crowd, until he stood eye to eye with a gray mare. Her forelock and mane were braided with gold and purple ribbons, and over her back she wore a gold and purple body cloth. What little he could see of her neck and legs was a sheen that told of endless currying.

Grudgingly he thought, "You're something to look at." But aloud he said, "Beauty is as beauty does."

"Hey, men!" a gruff voice mocked. "Listen here to the little preacher-boy. 'Beauty is as beauty does'!"

A roar of laughter went up on all sides. And all at once the day that had seemed so full of fun and frolic clouded over with doubt. Joel turned his back on the mare. He did not want to see her delicate head again. Nor did he care to look at the other Thoroughbred at all. He wanted only to get away from the crowd, to get back to the schoolmaster. But now the tide of men was turning, sweeping, and jostling him along. He was caught in the jam like a piece of drift. There was no choice but to inch ahead with the pulsing current of men.

At last the crowd began to fan out against a stone fence enclosing a pasture. And there to Joel's sudden joy he spied Little Bub calmly scratching his shoulder against a shellbark hickory tree. How hard and tough and courageous he looked! And how frisky and dear! In a flash Joel had leaped the fence.

Now he was hovering over the dusty creature, trying to comb the tangled forelock and mane with his fingers. He was like some fond parent wanting his young one to make as good a showing as any.

Robert Evans turned around from the nearby watering trough where he was scooping water to cool his brow. His face dripping, he strode over to Joel and picked him up by the seat of his pants. "You . . . you tomnoddy!" he bellowed, dropping the boy on the other side of the fence. "Leave the horse be. Scratchin' and grazin' will do him a heap more good than all your billin' and cooin'."

Red with shame, Joel picked himself up and ran to the inn. He was just in time to hear Mister Jenks call out: "Hey, Morgan! Yon cuckoo crows the hour of five. Where's that there New York Foppington and his fancy partner?"

All necks craned to look at the clock on the wall.

95

Each time the little bird popped out of its door and uttered its merry call, the crowd grew quieter and quieter until there was nothing to be heard but an echo dying.

Then, suddenly, every nose in the room twitched. An oversweet smell of pomade and lavender water penetrated the tobacco smoke. Again, with a single motion, all heads turned toward the stairway from which the scent came. There, mincing down the steps, came the bewigged gentlemen — Jonathan Foppington and his partner, the Honorable James Montague, Esquire. They wore flowered vests, and coats with long skirts that swayed with every movement. And their pumps were adorned with great silver buckles such as few of the Vermonters had ever seen.

When they reached the landing, both men stopped. Like actors in a play, each took a jeweled snuffbox from his waistcoat. Then, giving the lid a light tap, each opened his box, dipped into the snuff with a thumb and a forefinger, and carried a dainty pinch to his nostrils. "Ah-aah," they gasped, trying to encourage a sneeze. But no sound came. Only a sigh like that made by a bellows.

For a stunned moment the onlookers were as still as figures in a painting. Then clay pipes began puffing violently to rout the perfume smell, and everyone began murmuring at once.

Joel caught only scraps of talk. But the remark he liked the best was Seth Toothaker's. "High-duck dandies I calls 'em — them and their horses, too!"

Nor did the New Yorkers try to hide *their* feelings. They looked down their noses at the Vermonters in rough homespun. And later, when they went out to the pasture and saw Evans saddling up, they laughed until they had to mop their tears with lace-edged handkerchiefs.

"Hmph!" they snorted. "Is this the runty little thing we've been hearing about? 'Tis an insult to match our blooded horses against him." Then in a stage whisper meant for everyone's ears, Jonathan Foppington said, " 'Tis a well-known fact that horses with short necks can't run."

This was too much for Abel Hooper. He shook a long, horny finger at the New Yorkers and bawled out, "It may s'prise you gentlemen to know that this here horse ain't a-goin' to run with his *neck!* I and my mare, Nanny Luddy, can testify to that!"

The crowd burst into a fit of laughter. It was Vermont against New York now, and the men were all for Bub in spite of their wagers.

Out of the Satchel

BEAVER POND was as oval as an egg, and the margin of track around it was covered with fine turf. When the owners of the entries and their followers arrived at the track, they found it completely hemmed in by a great throng. A few seats were arranged, secure from danger, for the ladies. And at the starting line, which was also the finish, a small stage had been erected for the judges and the dandies from New York, and other prominent gentry. These included the famous Lightning Rod, Jr., grandson of Benjamin Franklin; and Samuel Adams, publisher of a journal in Boston; as well as a legislator, a councilor, and several other dignitaries.

After a whispered conference among the judges, Schoolmaster Morgan was also invited to sit on the stage.

Never had the Beaver Pond track known such excitement! The ladies were betting their gloves and copper half-cents, while the men wagered quarters and dollars, five to one against Little Bub.

Stealthily now Joel edged around behind the judges' stand. It wouldn't do to let the schoolmaster see him. His heart beating light and quick in his throat, he hurried to the oxcart, caught up the satchel, tucked it under one arm, and came running back to the starting line.

On either side of the stand there was a solid press of people. Joel had to get down on his knees and crawl between legs to reach the track. Two horses were approaching the starting post. At sight of them the men began to laugh and murmur. From his crouched position Joel looked out between a pair of dusty boots and saw why. It was a strange match indeed! One tall, satiny mare bearing a jockey in purple silks against a rough-coated work horse with a burly farmer on his back.

Joel's eyes flashed in indignation. Where was the other blooded horse? Did Little Bub have to race them one at a time? Did he have to run *two* races?

" 'Tain't fair!" he shouted, but his voice was lost in the din.

Now the starter came forward with a drum, and Joel smiled in spite of himself. Bub was not afraid of drums! For a full moment the starter, drumsticks upraised, looked to the judge, waiting. At last the judge nodded for the tap. And at that selfsame instant, Joel tore open his satchel, jerked out a little hound-dog, and did something he had never done before. He pinched the dog's tail as hard as he could and tossed him onto the course just as the tap of the drum sounded.

Like a streak of light the creature flew down the track, his yelpings lost in the cry: "They're off!"

Together the two horses sprang forward, but Morgan's horse shot ahead with a squeal. He was not in a race; he was hot in pursuit of his howling, noisy enemy, the Jenkses' hound! With every stride he drew his hind legs under him until they leaped ahead of his forelegs. He ran like whipcord, determined to get within striking distance, to rout the pesky nuisance.

Silvertail galloped hard to keep up, but the little horse had taken the lead from the start and there was never a duel between them. Even on the turns the Morgan held his lead. Now they were coming down the stretch with Silvertail fading. Horse sense must have told her she had no chance. The Morgan was increasing his lead . . . by two lengths . . .

by three lengths . . . by five. Now he and the yellow dog were crossing the finish line together! It was all Evans could do to pull him up. Three times he had to call "Whoa!"

Doubled over in joy, Joel thought he would never stop laughing. The tears rolled down his cheeks as he shouted breathlessly, "Bub wins! He wins!"

The roar of the crowd sounded like thunder in the mountain. The men who lost their bets clapped

and cheered just as loud as those who won. "Did you notice?" they whooped. "He just riz up and was off like a spring freshet!"

From the corner of his eye Joel saw Master Morgan starting toward him, and his laughter stopped short.

"Son!" the schoolmaster said as he drew close.

"Yes?"

"Was that the Jenkses' little yellow dog?"

"Yes, sir."

"If that was your surprise, I do not think much of it. Round him up at once and put him back in your bag."

"Yes, sir."

Joel moved off, almost bumping into Jonathan Foppington and Mister Montague. They brushed him roughly aside and grabbed the schoolmaster's arm.

"That yellow hound!" they raged, forgetting their fine manners. "Of all the mean, low-down, disgraceful, despicable, dastardly, scheming tricks!"

Master Morgan spoke soothingly. "I am sorry, gentlemen."

"Hark to the man!" James Montague turned to the crowd and mimicked the schoolmaster. " 'I am sorry,' the man says!"

"Aye. That I am, truthfully. And see? The boy Joel has caught the bewildered pup and is putting him away in the satchel. He will not interfere in the next race, I promise it."

Mister Montague snorted loudly into his handkerchief. "Come, Foppington, let us not consort with a trickster. Sweepstakes is a faster horse than Silvertail. The next race will be quite different."

The next race *was* different — even the start was different. The owners afoot — Jonathan Foppington and Justin Morgan — had the honor of leading their horses, mounted by their riders, out onto the track. Side by side they marched twenty paces behind the starting line. Then, as a pistol barked, they let go their hold and the two jockeys swung the horses around, applied their heels, and the race was on!

Sweepstakes, a shiny, long-legged black, and the Morgan got away to a fast start. For a dozen rods they ran neck and neck, the Morgan taking almost two strides to the black's one.

On the sidelines Joel bounced up and down, clucking to Bub, calling to him, coaxing him. "Come on, Bub! Do it double quick. Go it! Go it!"

And then at the first turn, just when the little horse was nosing for the lead, he threw a front shoe. Like some pinwheel it went arcing into the air, barely missing the white-wigged dandies. A big man ran back to capture it for a souvenir, while all the Vermonters groaned and suffered as if their own shoes had suddenly been wrenched off.

Joel's stomach churned. He started to shield his eyes, not wanting to look at Little Bub limping out the race, not wanting to see him stumble and fall behind.

But Little Bub was not limping! Joel could hardly believe what he saw. The Morgan had lost stride, had lost ground, but right there at the turn he seemed to know that he must take the lead again, now or never! It was as if the world were too small for them both and he knew it. Without help from Evans, he caught his stride and turned handily, making the Thoroughbred look clumsy as a camel. Bub's whole way of going said: "Hoofs were made before shoes. Weren't they!"

He began gaining on the big black as with one foot bare he flung himself forward like some wild thing, his short legs pumping so fast they blurred. Ears laced back, he inched up on Sweepstakes. Faster, faster, faster. The goal just ahead now.

"Come on, Bub!" Joel yelled.

And in the stand the schoolmaster was clapping Lightning Rod, Jr., on the back, crying, "Look at Bub! He's a blue streak of wind!"

A roar went up from the crowd as the little horse crossed the finish line, the winner by half a length.

Sweepstakes, winded and lathered, was led back to the stables. He looked like a defeated horse. The Morgan, however, acted almost joyful. He arched his stocky neck, swiveled his ears, and calmly gazed at the waving, yelling throng. He seemed to know the cheers were for him, and unashamedly he enjoyed them.

"Grit!" shouted Nathan Nye. "That's what he's got. Why, he run two races to their one. Them high-duck horses was all pampered like hothouse flowers. They didn't have a chance."

It was a curious fact, but the gentlemen from New York did not try to buy Little Bub. "He's a freak," they smiled thinly. "Bound to break down any day." They paid the schoolmaster the fifty-dollar purse, and as quickly as they could, disappeared into the inn. It was plain to see they wished only to get away from the gay and happy crowd, especially from that gleeful young apprentice boy.

On their way home in the starlight, Joel and the schoolmaster and Mister Jenks were too tired for much talk. They jounced along, each tasting his own memories. The little hound-dog snored contentedly in Joel's lap, the worries of the day forgotten.

When almost home, the schoolmaster reached out and tucked ten silver dollars into the boy's hand. "Five are for you, lad, and five for Evans. You'll be seeing him before I do."

Joel felt of the big coins in wonder, tracing his finger over the woman's head with her hair flying — like Little Bub's mane. He had seen plenty of silver dollars at the inn, but these were the first he had held for his own.

"Do you know?" he said with a little sigh of happiness. "I reckon now I can buy Little Bub when my term is done and I'm free. Miller Chase has promised to give me a new suit of clothes then, but I aim to ask for the money instead. And with these dollars besides, why, I'll be able to buy Bub as easy as anything!"

"He'll be old then, lad, and you'll be man-grown."

Joel only half heard. It never occurred to him that Little Bub would some day be an old horse. The years ahead seemed like nothing. Nothing at all. In just a short time he would own the fastest horse in Vermont! A shiver of joy passed through him. "Master Morgan," he said with a fierce gladness, "things be working out just fine!" And he patted the little hound-dog because he felt good toward the whole wide world.

"Things are working out fine for me, too, Joel! I

can pay off my debts now, and it seems I can almost hear our new harpsichord sounding out in the schoolhouse."

They rode on in silence, the schoolmaster and the boy each remembering that early morning when Little Bub turned out of Farmer Beane's gate and came along, uninvited.

Bub Travels the Singing Circuit

By autumn Little Bub's term of rental was up, and scarcely had Robert Evans returned him to Master Morgan when horse traders came knocking at the schoolhouse door. They were greedy for the little horse, and one afternoon the talk drifting out the windows sounded as if an auction were going on.

The schoolmaster could not help smiling, but he shook his head to everyone. Now he had need for a horse. Instead of teaching in Randolph only, he was

109

to be a traveling singing master for all the schools in mid-Vermont.

Even to Horse-trader Hawkes, who made the best offer of all, he said No. "I do not need the money now," he explained. "We have a nice harpsichord in the school, and my debts are all paid up, except to a lad named Joel Goss. If I use the horse gently, he *may* live long enough to pay that debt too. Meanwhile, Bub can carry me around on my singing circuit."

Thus began for Little Bub a whole new life — a life of joyful ease. Justin Morgan weighed only half as much as Robert Evans, and as he rode from school to school, he allowed Bub to set his own pace — walk or trot or canter, as it pleased him. By and by he trusted Bub so completely that he would drop the reins, write a few bars of music and lustily sing the tune as he jogged along.

Then while Master Morgan gave his singing lessons, Bub was not even tied to a hitching post. The schoolyard was his! He could kick his heels or roll in the grass with all the freedom of a colt. Sometimes white dandelion blowballs or milkweed fluff got into his nostrils, tickling the hairs until he snorted and sneezed them away. But when the wind was still, he lay still, too, just dozing in the warm sunshine and listening to the children sing their do-re-mi's.

The moment that he heard the scuffling of feet in

the cloakroom, he was up in a flash, waiting at the schoolhouse door. As the children came tumbling out, he was there to greet them, pawing the air with a forefoot as if to say, "I'm here! I'm here! You knew I'd be here!"

He seemed to have a special liking for tow-headed boys, nosing them over as if they pulled some trigger in his mind. But boys and girls both clamored to pet him and to feed him apples and horehound candy.

Little Bub thrived on his new way of life. His days were all the same, and all were good. There were grass and hay aplenty, and cooling streams in which to splash, and sun-dappled roads to travel, and music the livelong day. It was a good life, this life on the singing circuit.

But just when Bub had learned the way to all the towns and knew all the children, his easy days came to a sudden end. One morning at Woodstock, Vermont, Master Morgan felt too ill to teach. He barely reached the home of his friend, Sheriff Rice, when he had to be helped out of the saddle and carried into the house.

Even though the schoolmaster was well up in years, the Rices cared for him and his horse as if they were both children in need. They saw to the master's peace of mind, too. They sent word to all of his schools, and to the boy at Chase's Inn.

It was a traveling peddler, carrying clocks and

firearms, that brought the news to Joel. "Mister Rice says to tell ye the schoolmaster has the lung fever, but he'll be writing ye a letter almost any day." And he laid a kind hand on the blond head when he saw the boy struggling with an inner tumult of tears.

From that time forward Joel always ran out to meet the mail coach as it swung into the yard every fortnight. But in the small bundle of letters that the driver held out, there was never one for him. He waited months to hear, and then, all of a sudden, the letter appeared in Mistress Chase's hands. She was holding it against the candlelight early one morning when he came down to kindle the fire.

"Never knew a letter to bring *good* news," she snapped, "and bad news means sloven work — or none at all. Time enough to read this when your chores be done."

Then she tossed the letter onto the bar counter, and sat down at her spinning wheel, eyeing the boy like a cat waiting for a mouse to make a false move.

A wordless fear hung over Joel as he did his work. He scoured the pewter, seeing in the shine of it the schoolmaster's tired face and Little Bub's frisky one. And he pounded a patch over the worn spot in the porridge kettle, hearing hoofbeats in the sound of the hammer. Then he worked on dully — scrubbing the floor, sanding it, chopping firewood, bringing in water — trying not to think as he worked.

Now at last he was done. Now, as on other days, he should be at the sawmill. He took a step toward the counter. "Now, ma'am?" he asked.

Mistress Chase looked up from her spinning. "Whittle me a new butter paddle first. Then ye can read that letter, and if'n ye got any cryin' to do, ye can do it at the sawmill."

Obediently Joel set to work, but his mind could not be controlled. He tried to shut out all the terrors and troubles that the letter might hold — the schoolmaster worse, Little Bub fallen sick . . .

"Oh, drat it!" Mistress Chase broke into his thoughts. "Likely the paddle'd be no-account anyway. Fergit it, boy. I don't know what makes me so cantankerous. Go read yer letter and tell me what's in it."

Joel's hands swooped for the letter. Then two at a time he climbed the ladder steps, and in the quiet of the little garret room he opened it up and pored over each word.

Woodstock, Vermont
23 April 1798

Joel, lad:
The Rice family here in Woodstock have been nursing me these many months. Now once again I am in debt — to the doctor for visits and bloodlet-

tings, and to the chemist shop for pills and physics and blisters.

I could, of course, sell Little Bub and have enough and more to pay up all I owe, for he is a valuable stallion now, and his colts much sought after. But he has become dear to my heart, too. Moreover, you will be happier, I know, if I leave him to the Rices, who have been so kindly to him, and to me. They, in return, will pay my bills. Mister Rice is Sheriff of Woodstock and can use a horse to good purpose in apprehending thieves and miscreants.

Our Bub is in fine fettle, lad — sound of barrel, glossy of coat, and flashy of eye.

When you are freed of your apprenticeship, you will then find a way to take care of him. I pray that day may come soon, for as Farmer Beane would say, you and Bub fit together snug as two teaspoons. Even Mister Rice has told me full many a time as he fed me a gruel or a pudding that whosoever gentled the creature had done a most able job.

When some traveler from here is headed Randolph way, Mister Rice will ask him to take to you my songbooks and whatever of my clothes are still wearable.

Do not feel sorrow for me, lad. I welcome rest and peace. If my final pilgrimage be as pleasant as our junket with the colts, I shall be happy.

Good-night, dear Joel, and God bless you.
I am,
Your friend,

Justin Morgan

Joel tried to read the letter again, but the words began to weave and blur into each other, and then he couldn't see them at all.

His feet found the ladder and took him down, and for want of his mother he sobbed unashamedly on Mistress Chase's bosom.

The Auction Block

No one knew quite how it happened, but after Justin Morgan died, his full name was given to the little horse. When Joel heard about it, he was glad. "The schoolmaster'd be proud to fasten his name on Bub!" he said.

The slow seasons wore on. Summer and the high sun making shimmers of heat along the fields. Winter with indigo shadows riding across the snow. Spring moving in, with pale blossoms and wild bees humming. Then summer again. Around and around went the seasons, while the schoolmaster's horse served the Sheriff of Woodstock. Then one day

Robert Evans went to the Sheriff, wanting to buy the little stallion. To Evans' astonishment, Mister Rice nodded.

"My days as sheriff will be done, come July," he said, "and a horse be a luxury I can no longer afford. Besides, the critter actually grows stronger as I grow weaker — fer a fact, man! My bones is getting too old and creaky to go galloping over the countryside on a spunky stallion like him."

Robert Evans had land of his own now, and Justin Morgan was soon back in harness, working the sun up and working it down. What amazed Joel, and everyone else, was that instead of growing thin and poor with work, he grew stout and sturdy. He seemed to work for the *fun* of it, as if he enjoyed the very sounds and smells of work — tug chains going jingle-jangle, sledge runners squeaking over frozen snow, and the misty-moisty fragrance of freshly turned earth.

He took each morning as it came. And at twilight, when he should have been bedded down for the night, he was used by one or the other of Mister Evans' family. Often Mistress Evans with a tiny baby on her lap drove him to a quilting party. Then he stepped along ever so carefully. He seemed to know she was a timorous soul.

But if Amantha, the eldest daughter and a natural-born horsewoman, rode him to town, he galloped fast and bold, like some high-mettled Thorough-bred.

Neighbors, admiring these qualities in Justin Morgan, now brought their mares to him to be bred. The colts he fathered sometimes took on the color of the dam, but there all likeness to her stopped. The bold eye, the closely-coupled body, the easy gaits, the honest disposition were all Justin Morgan's.

In spite of the horse's help, Robert Evans failed to make his farm pay. And one day Justin Morgan was up for sale in front of the Sheriff's office in Randolph.

Joel was helping a journeyman saddle his horse behind the inn when he heard the news.

"Fer land's sake, boy, is the horse anything to ye?" the man asked as he saw Joel turn pale.

"Aye, sir. 'Twas me who gentled him. And 'tis me who wants to buy him."

"You don't say! Well, come along, lad. We can ride double, and I'll drop ye off at the auction block."

Joel ran quickly into the inn and came out clutching his five silver dollars. This was the first time he had ever left without his master's permission. But there was not a moment to lose. Once Little Bub was his, he thought as he climbed up behind the journeyman, Miller Chase would be glad! He could help in the logging and in ever so many ways.

118

"Please, sir," Joel urged, "could you jiggle the lines and hurry your mare along?"

The journeyman clucked, and the old mare responded with a listless trot. "You figure the miller'll let you keep a horse?" came the friendly question.

"Yes, sir." Joel gulped. "That is . . . I'm pretty sure, sir."

The Sheriff himself was leading Bub onto the auction block when Joel arrived.

In the front row of a big gathering a moon-faced man waddled forward. "One silver dollar's my offer," he said in a rough, croaking voice.

"I have one dollar. I have one dollar," the Sheriff's voiced intoned. "Who'll make it two?"

"I'll make it two!" came Joel's quick cry. In his mind he saw the big man astride, weighting Little Bub down until his back went sag and ugly.

The Sheriff's jaw fell open. "Wal . . . wal!" he exclaimed. "A bound boy makes it two dollars. I have two dollars. I have two dollars. Who'll make it ten?"

The moon-faced man raised three fat fingers.

"Three dollars I'm offered. I have three dollars. Who'll make it . . ."

"Three dollars and a half." Joel's voice had eagerness in it now. No one else seemed to be bidding, and he still had money left.

"Four and a half!" laughed the moon-faced man.

"Five . . . please." The thin voice sank.

And now all around Joel other voices were raised — brisk, confident voices, making big fine bids. The boy looked down at the five dollars in his hand, and they seemed to shrink and shrivel, like bacon over a hot fire. He tried to pinch off the tears that grew out of his disappointment. He folded his pocket handkerchief — the one the schoolmaster had left him — around the dollars and put them inside his shirt. Then he made his way over to the auction block, where the little horse stood, small and brave.

"Feller," he said low-voiced, "reckon you can't understand why I don't buy you. Eh?"

The Morgan funneled his ears toward Joel. Then he reached out with his nose to gather in the boy's scent. A whicker of recognition escaped him.

"Listen, feller," Joel whispered, while the bidding went higher and higher, "next time I'll have a pocketful of money. See if I don't! And I'll give you a green meadow with a creek snakin' through it. And I'll give you a fine stable with a thick bed of straw. And I'll give you sweet hay, and all the corn and oats you should eat. And I'll give you a blanket in winter. And I'll rub you proper night and morning."

When he could think of nothing more to give, he ran his strong hands over the horse's muscles, and then felt of his own. "Hard as flint," he nodded. "Yes, 'tis just as I said! You and me's growing big together . . . well, *almost* together," he added with a twisted smile.

"Joel!"

The boy turned around to face Miller Chase.

"Knew I'd find ye here. We both got to hyper on home now, or the missus'll want a lot o' explainin'."

"But the bidding," Joel said. " 'Tain't over. We got to know who buys Little Bub!"

"We'll know all right, son. Bein' landlord of an inn has got advantages. 'Tain't nothing we don't hear — sometimes afore it happens!"

Miller Chase was right. That evening the inn was lively as an anthill with comings and goings.

"Ye should've heard the bidding!" Nathan Nye said, thumping a new arrival on the back. "It waxed a-hotter and a-hotter until a carpenter laid down sixty-five dollars in hard money and led the horse away."

But what Mister Nye did not know was that in walking Justin Morgan home, the carpenter was stopped by a darkeyed stranger. With a few glib words, the man forced twelve gold pieces worth ten dollars each into the carpenter's hands. Then quick as a wink, he unhooked the halter, bridled the Morgan, and rode off, bareback, into the red ball of the sun.

The carpenter, mouth agape, stood all alone on the road, stood holding the gold pieces in one hand and a limp rope in the other.

Little Bub Lost

It was unbelievable, this thing that had happened. Justin Morgan dropped out of Joel's life as completely as if he had been swallowed by quicksand. No one seemed to have any knowledge of his whereabouts.

In desperation the boy stopped every traveler who came to Chase's Inn, and carefully described the horse. "Reddish brown," he would say, "without any white markings at all. And his ears be extra small but pricked sharp. And he's less'n fourteen hands high, but he's *big* for his size," he would add pridefully.

Always the answer was the same. "Sorry, young feller, I call to mind big beasts aplenty, but no little critter like you describe."

Almost daily Joel questioned Robert Evans and the carpenter, until both men hid behind any convenient object to avoid the boy's eyes. He pestered Nathan Nye, too, and Mister Jenks and Mister Fisk. He even wrote to Jonathan Foppington in New York, but no answer came.

Months passed, and only garbled stories reached the inn: Justin Morgan was in the hands of a kindly blacksmith in Burlington, a cruel bricklayer at Montpelier, a horse breeder at Ryegate. However, by the time the rumors were traced, the little horse had always moved on again, leaving only his colts behind.

Several times, in tracking down clues, Joel was asked if he wouldn't like to buy one of these colts instead. At Ryegate he was tempted by an especially appealing foal with the Morgan look so strong in him that it made Joel catch his breath. Then the little one neighed, a kind of weak flutter, and Joel found himself thinking back to Bub's vigorous bugling, and he found himself living over again the long trip home from Springfield, and the night after night when he rode Bub over the hills, and the weeks and the months of gentling.

"No, thank you, sir," he said to the horse breeder, "I'll just keep a-lookin'."

In spite of each disappointment, his faith never wavered that he would some day find the Morgan. And with each disappointment Miller Chase drew closer to Joel. "Tell ye what, son. When your days as apprentice be over with, I'll take ye on as partner. I'll even let ye build a barn of yer own behind the mill and raise colts . . . that is, if ever ye should find him."

Often in imagination Joel was in his own rough-made stable. He would be chewing on a wisp of sweet-smelling hay, while outside a spring rain drummed on the roof, and inside, three brood mares nursed their foals. What tickled Joel the most was that in the far stall the Morgan looked on, big-eyed and proud.

What did it matter if in the midst of Joel's dream Mistress Chase snapped a dish towel smartly across his cheek and gave her opinion of apprentices who had only half a mind on their work? Joel felt neither the sting of the towel nor the sting of the words, for the dream persisted.

Days stretched out into long years. War came, and it tapped Joel on the shoulder. By this time he was no longer an apprentice. He was a young man now, working as partner to Miller Chase, and he was free to enlist. The reasons for the war were only half clear to him. He had heard that British seamen were scrambling aboard American ships and forcing American sailors to help fight Napoleon. He had heard, too, that the English were threatening freedom of the seas. And so, on June 18, 1812, when the men in Washington declared war on Great Britain, Joel figured they probably knew what they were doing.

When his thoughts were on war, he tried hard to think of the important things at stake. But he kept seeing the horses instead, seeing them charge into battle, face gunfire, seeing them fall half dead on the field with bullet wounds, and no one to care for them. What if Little Bub were one of the wounded? Or what if he were the mount of some ruthless officer who cast him aside for a fresh horse rather than water and feed him?

Joel was like a man with a fire burning inside him. His mind was made up. There was a small mounted force in the Vermont militia, and he would join it. But he would not go empty-handed, for he knew of the desperate need for all kinds of supplies.

While other volunteers were saying long good-byes with feasting and laughter, Joel worked and dripped sweat. He went from house to house, chopping wood, scrubbing and sanding floors, cleaning out stables, doing any task at all, if only the housewife would give him a wool blanket or a water bucket in return.

"Warmth and water — that's what wounded horses need!" he explained.

When Joel had collected a goodly supply, he presented himself to the first sergeant of the small division of cavalry stationed at Rutland. The sergeant, a shoeing smith, was a jovial fellow, squatty as an apple tree, with shining seed-like eyes almost lost in wrinkles and folds.

"Sergeant!" Joel said, then stopped to put down the big bundle of freshly washed blankets and the stack of buckets. He remembered suddenly to salute.

The smith returned the salute in amusement, but his eyes were busy, looking over the much-needed equipment, sizing up the earnest young man. He hooked his thumbs in the belt of his leather apron.

"Reckon you had more to say, son?" The words chuckled out, as if whatever the young man had to say would be good.

"Sergeant!" Joel began a second time. "I understand you doctor the sick and disabled horses, and shoe the healthy ones."

The smith nodded his bald head and smiled into the serious eyes.

Joel hesitated. "Could I . . . that is . . . could
126

I help? I've a hankering to work with horses," he added quickly, without explaining why.

"Let's try you out, then!" And the smith heaved a great sigh, muttered a prayer, and bent down to gather up the blankets.

"I'll Go to Plattsburg!"

THE EARLY DAYS of the war were strangely quiet for
Joel, and for all Vermont. With most of the fighting
on the high seas between gunboats and frigates, the
foot soldiers and cavalry were not called into action.

An uneasiness lay on Joel at the utter sameness
of his days. Groom stout horses. Groom ribby ones.
Clean and oil saddles and bridles. Wash blankets.
Help the smith with a colicky animal, help him shoe
a nervous one. Joel tried to make believe that each

horse was Little Bub and so do a better job. But it was no use. These creatures were as unlike Justin Morgan as water is unlike wine.

As the slow days dragged by, Joel tried to reason with himself. "Maybe Bub wouldn't know me if I did find him, and maybe I wouldn't know him." Yet all the while he could see the purple-brown eyes, and feel the lips nuzzling at his neck, and hear the funny neigh that started out so high and fierce and pinched off into a rumbly snort.

"Sergeant," he said one night as he lay sleepless on his cot in the smith's tent, "this be a half-hearted war! If I had my 'druthers, I'd ruther be in the fight or else stayed to home."

The smith was sitting cross-legged before the open flap of the tent, smoking and looking out into the starry night. He took his pipe from his mouth and faced around to Joel. His words came hard and fast-spoken. "The tide has turned, son. Ye may as well know the worst — the British are fixin' to attack New York State! Why, this very moment they're swingin' down from Canady at such a pace that Colonel Totten up in Plattsburg is cryin' out for help."

Joel sat bolt upright. The blood pounded hotly through him. "What we waiting for, sir?"

"For Governor Chittenden to make up his mind."

"What's holdin' him back?"

"Conscience, mebbe."

129

"Conscience!" Joel choked out the word.

"Aye. He don't feel he's got a right to send our militia out of Vermont."

"But, sir, Plattsburg's only a whoop and a holler across Lake Champlain!"

"Aye. And my guess is that the Governor might be layin' awake this minute, making a mighty important decision."

The smith's prophecy came startlingly true. In the dark watches of the night Governor Chittenden relented, and while he still would not order the militia to Plattsburg, he did not forbid the men to go.

When morning came, how they cheered the news! All up and down the ranks hands went up and voices shouted, "I'll volunteer!" "I'll go to Plattsburg! I'll go!" Even the horses neighed as if they, too, welcomed action.

The town of Plattsburg sat perched on high ground overlooking Lake Champlain and the Saranac River. When Joel and his troop of men and mounts arrived, they found a battleground in the making. On a spit of land jutting out between the river and the lake, blockhouses and forts, storehouses and a hospital had already been built, and now the dirt was flying from trenches being dug.

Meanwhile, out in Plattsburg Bay, four American frigates were riding at anchor, their flags spanking in the breeze.

A September haze hung over land and water, and Joel felt as if it were charged with suspense, ready all in a moment to ball up into thunderclouds and rain down rockets of fire.

The feeling of excitement and danger grew in him as he learned that, even with Vermonters, there were only four thousand Americans to face fifteen thousand British — fifteen thousand veterans, fresh and jubilant from their victory over Napoleon. Already the news had leaked out: The British are coming — marching down from Montreal, steady of pace, steady of purpose, some afoot, some mounted. Fifteen thousand strong!

The American plan of action had leaked out, too, and the men, instead of being filled with terror, were full of eagerness to try it. Two roads led into Plattsburg from the north, one the Dead Creek Road that hugged along Lake Champlain, and the other the Beekmantown Road a few miles inland. Colonel Totten's plan was to divide his small army and send them northward to annoy and delay the enemy until the trenches were finished. Up the Beekmantown Road he sent the regulars, and up the Dead Creek Road he sent Colonel Appling with the mounted riflemen from Vermont.

As his platoon jogged north along the lake road, Joel thought he heard an oncoming sound. Could it be the first rumblings of thunder, or the muffled tap of drums? He thought he heard it, and then he

131

knew he heard it, above the hoofbeats of the horses. A rolling boom of noise! Now he saw movement — denser than cloud shadow, brighter than autumn leaves. The Redcoats!

"Open fire!" came Appling's sharp command.

Joel felt his mount tremble beneath him, felt his own rifle add to the fierce volley as if someone else had pulled the trigger.

With a crack of musket fire the marching British replied, while from their guns, hidden in the hills, screaming bombs and hissing rockets rained down on the Americans. To their amazement, the British saw the Americans fall back as if the volley of fire had overpowered them!

But already the Colonel's plan was beginning to work. Deliberately the Americans were bewildering the British. Deliberately they were challenging and vexing them by hindering their drive. They felled trees across the road, and broke up bridges as they withdrew.

The temper of the British rose to the boiling point. Their triumphal march had been spoiled by these stubborn Americans! They had to stop to heave the big trees aside, and they had to build makeshift bridges, while time spent itself.

All the way along, the Vermont cavalrymen annoyed the British veterans, coaxing them, teasing them down, down Dead Creek Road and into Plattsburg. When at last they were there, the Americans clattered across the final bridge to the safety of the peninsula. Then they destroyed that bridge, too, while the ships in the bay welcomed them with loud and mighty salvos.

Joel's heart thumped wildly as he saw that the regulars on the Beekmantown Road were now crossing and destroying the upper bridge and joining forces with them on the little spit of land. "It worked!" he shouted to himself. "The plan worked!"

But the real test of the few against the many was still to come. Across the river, the two armies — British and American — now eyed each other like cats ready to pounce. The American was the hunting cat, waiting. The British waited, too, waited for the Royal Navy to come sailing into Plattsburg Bay to give added strength and courage.

An hour went by, two hours, three hours. Joel tried to study the horses tethered across the river, but they were so many blobs with sticks for legs. Dusk closed in like a fog. The day went by. Then night and morning and brassy noon, and night again. Two days, three days, with only an occasional rattle of musket fire from both sides. Four days. Five days, while dry leaves lazied to earth and the sun set and rose, and men and mounts grew restive.

But on the sixth day a flotilla of British sloops and gunboats sailed regally into the bay. Suddenly the world was all noise and flame as the gunboats opened fire on the American ships.

At the same moment the British troops on land began their attack. Using planks and barrel staves for rafts, they tried to cross the Saranac, to climb up the steep banks of the peninsula.

"Follow me! Follow me!" Appling shouted as he wheeled his horse to meet the enemy.

Joel and the smith rode in tandem, following teams pulling gun caissons to the line of action. Their eyes were everywhere at once, on the teams, on the mounts up ahead. Horses stumbling or breaking into a crazy gallop were signals to them of bullet wounds or shell shock. Often before a horse fell, Joel had galloped to his side and caught the cheek strap of the frightened animal. Then he would tie the creature to a tree behind the lines where he would be out of danger.

All that morning of September 11 the land battle seesawed back and forth — first the British gained the river bank, then Appling's Vermonters raced up and fought them back.

But out in the bay the British were having the worst of it. Their fine vessels were splintering like matchboxes, tossing helter-skelter on the waves. By afternoon there was scarcely a gun in position. The captain, knowing the battle to be lost, ordered his vessels to strike their colors in surrender.

News of the surrender sent the Americans on land into a frenzy. They suddenly felt giant strong. Band after band let out whoops of joy. The sound was so loud it ricocheted to the hillsides and back again until it seemed as though untold numbers of new recruits had arrived. It was the clamor and shouting, as well as the Americans' spirit, that frightened and defeated the British on land.

To conceal their retreat, the British kept up a barrage of fire, but in the midst of it a black storm spilled from the heavens and poured down on the battlefield. In haste they abandoned their guns and fled. Only their dead and wounded, both men and horses, were left behind.

Now seemingly from nowhere came the American medical aides, their lanterns winking yellow in the rain. Colonel Appling sent for Joel and the smith to help with the wounded men of both armies. They improvised stretchers by thrusting muskets through coatsleeves, and they carried the wounded to the hospital building. All the while Joel worked, his mind kept remembering a mother robin who year after year built her nest on his window ledge. He remembered how she would hop onto the rim of the nest, worm in her beak, and whichever nestling squawked the loudest got the worm. It was the same on the battlefield, he thought: whichever man moaned the loudest was cared for first.

All night long Joel worked in the rain-soaked field, helping wherever help was needed. By midnight every wounded man was in the hospital. Then, at last, he could go to the horses. Suddenly new strength came into him and he felt his heart beat faster. What if one of the British horses were Justin Morgan? Dead or alive, he had to know.

The smith's weariness seemed to lift, too. "Joel!" he called out. "You handle the flesh wounds. I'll take the bad ones."

Joel worked quickly now. He filled an empty powder horn with alum, carrying it to the horses who, unlike the men, did not moan. In the thick darkness it was hard to tell the hump of a horse's body from a hummock of earth. He felt each mound carefully, letting his fingers tell him whether to stop and minister, or to go on. In the British sector he found a mud-slathered gray with a gaping wound in his thigh. With steady hand he poured alum into the wound, talking to the terrified animal as if it were a small child in trouble. He made himself look into the face of every horse, alive or dead, that he could find.

"I declare!" said the smith when they came together for a moment. "It puzzles me if 'tis the alum or your voice that stanches the blood and quiets the animals."

Toward morning the rain spent itself and a pale glimmer of dawn showed above the horizon. Joel, his work done, dropped down in exhaustion beneath a tree. Before he let sleep claim him, his lips formed a prayer of thanksgiving. "Dear God, I do thank thee that Little Bub weren't on the battlefield. But, O dear God, if it please thee," he whispered, "let me find him soon."

Then he pillowed his head in his arms and slept.

A Whinny in the Night

Soon after the battle of Plattsburg the war began to peter out. Both America and England realized they had nothing to fight over. With Napoleon captured and the bloodshed at an end in Europe, the very reasons for the war seemed to disappear. So the whole business was called off. It was almost as simple as that. There were no harsh terms for either side. Nothing but blessed peace.

News of the peace brought great rejoicing. The blockade along the Atlantic coast was lifted. The country began to build a great merchant marine. Men began dreaming of free public schools, of clean prisons, of putting an end to slavery, of settling new lands to the westward.

And in the little village of Randolph, too, progress was afoot. Joel was man-grown now, with a man's responsibilities. He was chairman of a committee to establish a free public library, and since his cavalry days even white-bearded men came to him for advice in doctoring their horses.

One bitter night in the dead of winter, Joel was on his way to the meetinghouse to discuss the new library. With his skates over his shoulder he stopped to pick up a neighbor, Ezra Fisk, Junior.

Usually the two talked and laughed as they skated up the river. But not this night. The wind blew howling out of the northeast, and a fine snow pricked their faces like so many needle points.

"We'll be getting a blizzard if this keeps up," Ezra yelled, turning his head to one side.

As they came to a bend in the river, Joel swerved to a sudden stop, listening. The wind had picked up a sound — a thin, high quaver. It was a sound that he knew in every part of him. It set his heart to hammering and started up an old aching inside him. "Could it be," he thought, "the wind is playing tricks? Or could it be the screaking of our skates mixed up in wind?"

And then, and then it came again — the high,

vibrating sound, blowing across him, into him, through his earmuffs, through his ears, into his mind. He tried to hold onto it, but the deep-toned thunder of the wind hurled it away.

"Ezra!" he shouted, skating wildly toward the figure pushing against the wind. He caught up to Ezra and spun around, bumping into him, sending him sprawling across the ice.

"Ezra!" he cried excitedly. " 'Twas the voice of someone I know."

The bewildered young man picked himself up, rubbing his elbow and knee by turns. "Voice or no voice," he muttered in annoyance, "be that fit reason for trying to break every bone in my body?"

But Joel had wheeled about and was off like an arrow. The sound had come from somewhere in the direction of Chase's Inn. In long, hard strides he was skating downriver, the way he had come. Through the whirl of snow he caught a prick of light ahead. He knew it for the familiar lantern on the shed behind the inn. He skated toward it, pulled by some seeming magnetism.

Behind him Ezra was calling, "Wait, you tarnal idiot! I want to see, too."

But now Joel was ripping off his skates, running and scrambling up the river bank, while the wind lashed at him and tore at his scarf and the heavy skates thumped against his body. He must get to

the shed quickly before the sound was lost to him forever. But even as he ran it came again, and Joel cried out, "I'm coming! I'm coming!"

He could see into the shed now, see each stall occupied. He grabbed for the lantern, but it was frozen to the peg. He worked it free, then hurried from stall to stall, lighting the face of each naimal. A white face. An iron gray. A chestnut, a brown, a bay. A broad-faced ox. Some had white stripes down their noses, and some had tiny snips or stars. But in all the long row there was not a face he knew.

Slowly, dejectedly, he returned the lantern to its peg, and said to the looming shadow that was Ezra, "I must've mistook that whinny for . . ."

There! It came again, the same thin flutter, the same high, trembling note.

Not waiting for the rumbling echo, not stopping for the lantern, Joel ran stumbling to the front of the inn. There, in the light pouring out the windows of the taproom, he saw a team of six horses hitched to a freight wagon. The horses looked all alike — gaunt, and old, and snow-matted. There was not a proud head nor an arched neck among them.

He rubbed his mittened hand across his eyes, trying to wipe away the wind-tears, trying to see more distinctly. He waited for his heart to stop pounding; waited, not knowing for what he waited. And then into the frosty night the high neighing started up again. Joel saw which horse moved, saw the head raise, saw the tiny ears swivel. It was the littlest horse in the team.

"Ezra!" he shouted. " 'Tis the wheel horse — the near one!"

In a flash he was holding the horse's face in his hands. "My poor Little Bub!" he whispered softly. "My poor, shiv'ring, starved Little Bub." He breathed on the tiny icicles that hung from the whiskers. Then he lifted Bub's hoofs, and with his fingernails began to dig out the frozen balls of snow, cursing the teamster who let his horses stand out on a night like this. As each ball of snow came loose, Joel stopped to breathe again on the icicles.

The little horse was trembling — not from cold, but from excitement. He tried to nicker, but all he could manage was a low whimper, like a child or a very old person. It seemed that he had spent himself in neighing, and now wanted only to rest his head in the warm, gentle hands. He nuzzled them feebly.

"Look, Joel! Look at the signboard!" cried Ezra, laughing. "These bags of bones have come to the right place."

The inn's signboard swung back and forth, creaking on its hinges. The last line, only a few inches above Little Bub, read: GOOD KEEPING FOR HORSES.

Joel's eyes seemed to strike sparks in the cold. "You ain't being funny!" he said angrily, as he pried the last ball of snow free. "And 'tain't easy to make you understand about this little horse. But I knew him when he could trot faster, run faster, and pull heavier logs than any horse in Vermont! 'Tis the Justin Morgan horse, Ezra. 'Tis the *Justin Morgan horse,* I tell you!"

The young man moved in closer. "This old beast the horse my father rented?" he cried in awe.

"The very one."

Now Ezra seemed angered, too. With his hand he

swept the snow from the horse's back. "Why, he's worn a harness so long it's almost grown on him! What in tunket we waiting for? Let's go in and tell that teamster a thing or two!"

Covering Little Bub with his coat, Joel gave him a final pat. "Please to let me handle this, Ezra," he said as he followed the young man into the inn.

At least a dozen men were gathered in the general room, eating and drinking and talking together.

"Gentlemen!" Joel addressed them in a stern voice he scarcely knew as his own. "Who is owner of the six-horse team at the hitching rack?"

"I am!" came a snarl from in front of the fire. "What's it to ye?"

Joel could see just the back of a chair, a coonskin cap showing above it, and two enormous feet beyond. The feet, in hobnailed boots, were stretched toward the hearth and a blazing fire.

As Joel and Ezra started toward the voice, one man tried to discourage them with a look. Another, older, got up from a bench and tugged at Joel's sleeve. "Better give him the go-by, feller," he said. "He's nasty as a polecat."

Joel shook his head. "I got this to do," he said, and strode over to the bulky creature.

The man seemed in a trance. The face was half hidden behind a shag of whiskers, and the yellow-green eyes stared straight ahead like those of an owl. Across the man's lap lay a bull-hide whip, and in
144

one hand he held a tankard of ale. The arm holding the ale waved the young man away, and the drink spattered and some of it struck the fire with a hiss.

Joel gazed at the whip and blurted out, "That wheel horse, the near one — what'll you take for him?"

The yellow-green eyes narrowed until they were no more than slits. Could this Simple Simon have meant the *littlest* horse?

Ezra, impatient with the delay, was stamping snow from his feet, and it made Joel think of the snowballs packed in Bub's hoofs. He repeated the question. Louder this time.

It was all the teamster could do not to laugh outright. For days he had been wondering how soon he would have to replace every horse in the hitch. And now someone wanted to buy the littlest one of all! He hunched forward in his chair, placed the tankard on the floor, and began flicking his whip, narrowly missing Joel's legs.

"Look-a-here, feller," his surly voice sounded out, "that little beast pulls better than the hull kit and caboodle. I wouldn't *hear* o' selling him. Nowise! Why, only a fortnight ago a man offered twenty dollar for him."

There was a shuffling of feet as everyone in the room gathered about. Joel turned away from the teamster. Breaking through the ring of men, he found Miller Chase. "Sir," he whispered earnestly, "the Morgan horse — he's right here at our hitching rack! That teamster owns him, and if I don't buy him tonight, sir, he may be dead in the morning. I got to have twenty-five dollars!"

Miller Chase was breaking a stick of cinnamon into a bowl of punch. He spooned it, thinking quickly and carefully before replying. At last he said, "Joel, lad, you are buying into my business, and you may be white-haired and old when it's all paid for. Times is hard. What's the sense getting deeper in debt on a nearly dead beast?" He looked up with kindliness in his eyes. "The Morgan must have considerable age on him, and don't you know he's liable to be rheumaticky and die soon?"

"Yes, yes, I know!" Joel spoke impatiently now. "But it's different with Little Bub, sir. He's a friend, and you don't turn down a friend just because he's old."

The miller smiled. And then as he caught sight of Mistress Chase sailing into the room, he lowered his voice. "All right, son, I'll loan you whatever it takes," he said, opening the cash box beneath the counter.

Joel felt the rough, gnarled hands close around his, felt the moneybag tucked into his palm. He tried to speak, but a choking filled his throat. Instead, he gripped the miller's hand in a clasp so hard it made the man wince. Then he went back to the teamster, who was slyly glancing around, wondering if he had lost his serious-eyed customer.

"I can offer you twenty-five dollars," Joel said, praying under his breath that it would be enough.

The huge man's eyes lighted greedily. "The crow-bait's yours!" he laughed as he pocketed the money and picked up his tankard of ale.

And so, at long last, Little Bub belonged to Joel.

Justin Morgan and the President

Joel had never known such warm and glowing happiness. He worked on Little Bub not only with hands and mind, but with heart and soul. While Little Bub slept, he walked around on tiptoe so as not to rouse him. Then he could hardly endure the waiting for him to wake up.

No human patient ever received more tender care. To coax his appetite Joel prepared steaming mashes of oats. And he thinned them with linseed tea for quick strength. He ground corn in his own gristmill, flavoring it with slices of crunchy carrots or rutabagas. He put a chunk of rock salt in his oat box, where Bub could lick a dozen times a day if he had a mind to.

At first the horse only lipped the food that Joel prepared and let it dribble from his mouth. But in a matter of days he was eating because he could not help himself. The soft mashes were so delicious and they required scarcely any chewing. He was like an invalid who wanted to make up for lost time. He ate and ate, while Joel looked on in delight.

As for drinking water, Little Bub could not seem to get enough of that, either. The teamster had expected him to eat snow or to break ice in a stream. But Joel warmed the bucket of water by the fire and enriched it with oatmeal.

In every move of Joel's there was life-giving warmth — in the rubdowns with his woolen mittens, in the flannel bandages that he wrapped about Bub's legs, in the melted sheep's fat with which he bathed the cracked hoofs. And there was coziness, too, in the way Joel tucked a fleecy blanket about him, pinning it in place close under the chin and belly.

It was like magic the way the little horse began to be himself again. His eyes livened, and his coat lost its harshness and took on a kind of luster. In time even the ribby look disappeared, and the hollow places at his flanks filled out. All Randolph began to notice the change. "I declare!" men said. "Justin Morgan is spry as a grasshopper!"

One early morning, some six months after he had found Little Bub, Joel cornered Mister Chase between piles of lumber in the millyard. "What I feel about Justin Morgan . . ." he said, and then he could not go on.

"What is it, son?"

Joel reached out and peeled off a splinter of wood, shredding it with his fingers. "What I feel," he burst out, "is that he ought to march in the big parade when the President of the United States comes to Vermont."

The miller laughed. "Well, you and me ain't going to argify about that. When's it to be?"

"A fortnight away — on the twenty-fourth, sir."

"Where at?"

"Burlington."

"Burlington!" The miller took off his hat and scratched his head. "Why, that's way up on Lake Champlain. Must be a good fifty mile, as the crow flies."

"That ain't no distance for a stout-hearted critter, sir. He can do it easy."

Mister Chase smiled at Joel. " 'Course he can. The Morgan's fine and fit as any horse in his prime. Anyways, I reckon you can decide, son. He's all yours."

Joel's laugh was deep and happy. "Why, so he be!" Then he added, "All the riflemen who served at Plattsburg will be there, too."

"And mebbe Joel hankers to polish up his buttons and be among 'em. Eh?"

"Mebbe so! But, sir, can you spare me?"

"By the great horn spoon, I ain't no Methuselah. You go, son. What's more, you see to it that Justin Morgan is spang up there in front where President Monroe kin see a horse what *is* a horse."

Two weeks later — on that sunlit morning of July twenty-fourth — there was a special kind of excitement in the air. In a pasture in Burlington, Joel was currying Little Bub as if his very life depended on it. Never before had Bub been groomed this carefully. It made his skin tingle and his blood race with well-being.

When his fetlocks had been trimmed, and the hairs in his ears and the whiskers about his chin, Joel stood back in admiration. "There!" he said with a final pat. "You even *look* like a parade horse. Do you know," he gazed into the liquid brown eyes, "you've just naturally growed young. Your heart be young, and so be you. In all the nineteen states I bet there ain't a finer horse! Now you graze, feller, whilst I suds myself in the creek behind the willows."

Joel's bath took far less time than the horse's.

Then on with the green coat and the white breeches, which had been washed and patched until they looked almost as good as new.

Now they were both ready. Now it was precisely eleven o'clock. Precisely the time to set out for Courthouse Square. As Joel rode up to the meeting place, his troop of cavalry was already gathering.

A shrill whistle pierced the air. Then, "Column of twos!" the Marshal of the Day shouted as he pumped his arm twice and held up two fingers.

Joel turned to look at the soldier beside him and broke into a grin. It was none other than the shoeing smith! As the columns moved forward, it seemed to Joel that all Burlington had turned out to watch the parade. A solid sea of people lined the streets from the courthouse to the college green. They began cheering the colors, cheering the soldiers, and they kept on cheering because they felt big and good inside.

Joel, too, swelled out in his chest as if this were more happiness than he could hold, for his Little Bub was surely the finest parade horse in the world. He acted as if he had been bred and born to parade. He answered the slightest pressure of Joel's knees. He kept in line obediently. On command, he walked backward; he walked sideways. And always his feet kept time to the beat of the drums.

Now they were approaching the President's stand, and from the church tower, bells began ringing — all softly solemn at first, then wild and merry until they sang up to heaven itself.

President Monroe, tall and erect, stepped forward on the stand, while a salute of guns shook the very earth. Many of the horses tried to wheel or bolt, but Justin Morgan did not flinch.

When the guns quieted and the bells stilled, the

153

people, too, fell silent, waiting. The President removed his hat and held it across his heart. His eyes looked straight ahead to a platform across the street. There, two hundred children in crisp pinafores and calico suits were on their tiptoes, ready to sing the new song, "The Star-Spangled Banner." Now into all that great quiet, a pitch pipe sounded, and at a signal from the teacher, two hundred treble voices sang out:

> "O say, can you see,
> By the dawn's early light,
> What so proudly we hailed
> At the twilight's last gleaming? . . ."

The President beamed all during the anthem, and when it was over, he bowed and clapped at the fine performance of the school children. Then, mounting a horse held in readiness, he rode between the columns of cavalrymen. Halfway down the line, the horse suddenly ducked his head between his legs. A bee had flown into his ear and was driving him frantic. He snaked his head along the ground and he reached up with a hind foot to scratch the buzzing thing away. It was all the President could do to dismount. A foot soldier had to lead the half-maddened horse away.

"Take my mount," a colonel offered.

"Take mine! Take mine!" voices went up on all sides.

The President smiled, and shook his head. He let his gaze travel up and down the columns as if he would continue his inspection afoot. But then his eye fell upon Justin Morgan and stopped there. He looked at the bright, intelligent face, and motioned to Joel to ride him out of line.

For one awful instant Joel could not cluck, or tighten his legs, or jiggle the reins. Every muscle seemed frozen. But at a good-humored nod from the President, his fright was gone. He leaped to the ground, and while a little murmur of surprise rippled down the columns, he presented Justin Morgan to James Monroe, President of the United States.

At first the little horse eyed the man in the tall hat as if he were the one to do the approving. Then, apparently satisfied, he bugled through his nose, those high quavering notes followed by a deep snorty rumble. It was almost as if he had said, "I *am* glad to meet you, sir!"

How the people roared in delight! It was like a storybook the way the Morgan seemed to understand the greatness of the occasion. He stretched so that the President could mount with ease. Then with Joel walking proudly behind, he moved on with lofty, cadenced action.

When the procession reached the college green, the President rode to a little knoll. It faced a natural amphitheater which was already filled with people sitting, and now with the followers of the parade, standing.

Colonel Totten, mounted on a white horse, was on the knoll, too. He raised his hand for quiet. "Ladies and gentlemen," his voice boomed slow and strong, "the President of the United States!"

A great hush fell. It was so still and respectful that a feeling of admiration for these people welled up in James Monroe. He was fingering the sheaf of notes in his pocket. But suddenly he changed his mind. This was no time for talking from notes; this was a time for talking from the heart. With one hand holding the reins and the other resting lightly on the Morgan's crest, he began:

"Fellow citizens! This picturesque scene is associated in every bosom with the highest honor of our country. The gallant action on your Lake Champlain bound the Union together by ties as strong as bands of steel."

A burst of applause filled in the little moment while the President took a breath.

"No nation has a richer treasure than liberty, and I am proud of the way American liberty was defended by the Green Mountain Boys. You citizens of Vermont are as firm as the mountains that gave you birth. May the bravery shown here ever animate your children to follow the glorious example of their forefathers!"

A thousand Vermonters cheered and threw their

hats into the air. This was a speech they liked — crisp and to the point, with no big-sounding words. The President smiled and bowed. He could not remember when he had been greeted with more hurrahs.

In the midst of all the rejoicing, Justin Morgan took it into his head to bow, too, and now the crowd went wild. It was hard to tell whether the Morgan or the President was the hero of the day!

Then the President dismounted, gave Justin Morgan a friendly pat, smiled his thanks to Joel, and handed him the reins.

Half the throng now followed the President down to the shore of Lake Champlain, where a steamboat waited to take him to Plattsburg. But the other half swarmed around Joel and Justin Morgan. There were professors from the college, and tradesmen, and all kinds of soldiers, and old ladies and young, and boys and girls, who now fumbled in pockets for good things to eat. They all wanted to go home and say, "I eenamost touched the President of the United States, but I really did feed the horse he swung up on!"

Some of the very farmers who had once poked fun at the Morgan's long tail were now trying to snip a few hairs for a souvenir. "I always knew he'd be a go-ahead horse!" they crowed.

Then, right there on the college green, questions began popping like sparks from a dry log. Who *is* the Justin Morgan horse, anyway? Who was his sire? Who was his dam?

In the midst of the din a white-bearded veteran from the Revolutionary War shouted for silence. "You folks be too young to remember," he bellowed, "but one black night during *my* war a fancy English Thoroughbred of the name of True Briton was hitched at a tavern near the British lines. Then along come a Yankee, and what did he do?"

"What?" chorused the crowd.

"Why, he stole that-there British horse and raced him across the lines. And 'twas him that sired Justin Morgan!"

"Sorry to contradict you, grandpap," a young man broke in, "but to my eye, he's got the build of them stout little pacers from Narragansett."

"Ye're wrong as a pump without a handle!" chirped a little cricket of a man. "He's a Dutch horse if ever I see one!"

"Begging your pardon," interrupted a very old lady, "I hearn from a good source that he's French Canadian."

The talk seesawed back and forth — first about the little Morgan's pedigree, then about his birthplace.

In the heat of the arguing, the shoeing smith rode up to Joel and motioned the crowd back. "Ladies and gentlemen," he announced, "Joel Goss here is the onliest one who knows about this horse. He, my friends, can answer your questions."

A silence came over the gathering as all eyes turned to Joel, who would rather have fought another battle than speak to such a large group. For courage he put an arm around Little Bub's neck and twined his fingers in the glossy mane. A sprig of evergreen from the horse's headstall fell to the ground just then, and at sight of it Joel thought of the Green Mountains and of his trip with the schoolmaster so long ago. The inheld words now came slowly, like raindrops from a tree long after the rain has ceased.

"When I was a knee-high boy," he said, taking a deep breath, "our singing master, Justin Morgan, took me with him to visit Farmer Beane down in Springfield."

"What's Farmer Beane got to do with it?" the same white-bearded veteran barked out.

"Just about everything," Joel explained. "Y'see, he owed the master a lot of money, but he didn't have any . . ."

"Go on!" the crowd urged. "We're follerin' ye."

"Well, the farmer didn't want to be beholden to anyone; so he gave the singing master a fine big colt named Ebenezer. And for good measure he threw in a mite of a colt called Little Bub.

"And that Little Bub . . ." Joel paused, smiling

awkwardly. "He be the one who took on the school-master's name, Justin Morgan."

"Go on, young feller," the old man prodded. "You're doin' fine."

"Well, the schoolmaster and Farmer Beane both be dead now," Joel said, restoring the piece of ever-green to the horse's headstall, "and likely nobody will ever know who was this fellow's sire and who was his dam. He was just a little work horse that cleared the fields and did what was asked of him."

Joel's face suddenly lit up as if he had thought of something for the first time. He spoke now to the horse, as though he were the one that mattered. "Why, come to think of it, you're just like us, Bub. You're American! That's what you are. American!"